DOCTOR WHO

2 new adventures

Also available:

Death Riders by Justin Richards

Heart of Stone by Trevor Baxendale

The Good the Bad and the Alien
by Colin Brake

System Wipe by Oli Smith

Alien Adventures
by Richard Dinnick and Mike Tucker

Coming soon:

Monstrous Missions
by Jonathan Green and Gary Russell

Step Back in Time
by Jacqueline Rayner and Richard Dungworth

Want to get closer to the Doctor
and learn more about the very best
Doctor Who books out there?

Go to
www.doctorwhochildrensbooks.co.uk
for news, reviews, competitions
and more!

BBC Children's Books

Published by the Penguin Group

Penguin Books Ltd, 80 Strand, London, WC2R 0RL, England

Penguin Group (USA) Inc., 375 Hudson Street, New York 10014, USA

Penguin Books (Australia) Ltd, 250 Camberwell Road, Camberwell,

Victoria 3124, Australia (A division of Pearson Australia Group PTY Ltd)

Penguin Group (NZ), 67 Apollo Drive, Rosedale, North Shore

0632, New Zealand (A division of Pearson New Zealand Ltd)

Canada, India, South Africa

Published by BBC Children's Books, 2011

Text and design © Children's Character Books

Terminal of Despair written by Steve Lyons

The Web in Space written by David Bailey

Cover illustrations by Kev Walker and Paul Campbell

ISBN – 978-14059-0-768-2

Mixed Sources
Product group from well-managed
forests and other controlled sources
www.fsc.org Cert no. SA-COC-1592
© 1996 Forest Stewardship Council
FSC

Printed in Great Britain by Clays Ltd, St Ives plc

DOCTOR WHO

2 new adventures

SIGHTSEEING IN SPACE

STEVE LYONS   DAVID BAILEY

CONTENTS

THE WEB IN SPACE

DOCTOR WHO

TERMINAL OF DESPAIR

STEVE LYONS

CHAPTER 1
ARRIVALS

'I think we've landed in an airport,' said Amy. The Doctor peered out of the TARDIS from behind her. 'Oh,' he said. 'Sorry about that. Come back inside. I'll try again. Better luck next time.'

'Er, not so fast if you don't mind,' said Amy. 'We're here now. What's wrong with having a quick look around?'

They were in a long, well-lit hallway. It was lined with luggage carousels. Most of these were still, but the one at the far end was turning. It was carrying a lone black sports bag around in endless circles.

The Doctor frowned. 'You want to see more

of this? Why?'

'Because it might be interesting, that's why,' said Amy. 'What do you have against airports?'

'Not only airports,' said the Doctor. 'It's bus stops, train stations, ferry terminals. Anywhere that people gather and just... *wait*.'

'Right,' said Amy. 'I get it.'

'They're hardly places at all really, are they?' said the Doctor. 'They're the places between other places – more interesting places. Isn't that right, Rory?'

Amy's husband had appeared in the TARDIS doorway. He looked nervous. Rory wasn't as comfortable travelling in space and time as the others were.

'You know, Doctor,' said Amy, 'people do use public transport. We can't all go whizzing about the universe in a super-duper police box.'

'Why is there no one around?' asked Rory.

The Doctor gave a disinterested shrug. 'Maybe it's night-time and there are no flights till morning. Maybe they've closed this terminal.'

'You said we'd landed in an airport, right?' said Rory. 'I heard you say that.'

He had noticed something the Doctor and Amy hadn't. Almost hidden behind the TARDIS, there was a small, round window. It looked out upon a vista of stars.

Amy saw it now too, and she grinned with excitement.

'I don't think we're in an airport,' said Rory.

'Space,' said Amy. 'We're in space. So, this must be a *spaceport*!'

'I can hear voices,' said the Doctor.

They followed the sound, until Amy said, 'I can hear them too.'

They passed through a security gate, which was open and unmanned. Then they came into a huge, open area, full of red plastic seats. There were scores of people – ordinary human beings – in there, milling about.

'This'll be the departure lounge, then,' said Rory.

The lounge was dominated by a curved outer wall. It was studded with airlock doors and portholes, through which they could see space again.

Great spaceships floated behind three of those portholes. They were attached to the airlocks by thick, white tubes.

'There,' said the Doctor, 'do you see now? All these people, and not one of them wants to be here. They all want to be somewhere else.'

'They do all look pretty miserable,' said Rory.

'I don't blame them,' said Amy. She pointed to a monitor, which hung from the ceiling. 'Look at the departures board. Every flight out of here is delayed.'

'Delayed, you say?' said the Doctor. 'How interesting. No, really, I think that's incredibly interesting. I'm so glad we came here and saw that. Now, can we leave?'

He turned and marched back the way they had come. He stopped when he saw that his friends weren't following him.

Amy had spotted a bright yellow shop sign at the far end of the lounge. It read: TERMINAL 4000 DUTY-FREE STORE.

'We have got to see in there,' she said. Noticing the Doctor's sulky expression, she pleaded, 'Ten minutes. No, five, tops. Come on, Doctor, we're in the future. I just want to see what a duty-free shop looks like in the future.'

The Doctor sighed and nodded. 'Five minutes,' he said.

'You heard the man, hubby dearest. Let's go!' Amy took Rory's hand. She dragged him after her as she ran to the shop.

The Doctor was still bored.

He paced up and down. He clicked his tongue impatiently.

He wondered how long his friends had been gone. He checked his watch. It had been almost a minute.

Someone had left an old paperback book on one of the plastic seats. It was a whodunit. The

Doctor liked whodunits.

He sat down, picked up the book and began to read. He skimmed the first three pages. He stopped and frowned. He flicked to the last page of the book, glanced at it and sighed. 'I knew it,' he said to himself.

A woman was standing nearby, watching him.

'Hello,' said the Doctor.

She looked surprised that he had noticed her. 'Hello,' she said, approaching the Doctor shyly.

The woman was young, with short, dark hair. She wore a red and purple uniform. 'I'm the Doctor,' said the Doctor, 'and you must be...?'

'Janie Collins,' said the woman. 'I'm a flight attendant with Orion Spaceways. I haven't seen you here before.'

'No. That's probably because I haven't been here before. I'm just passing through, really. You aren't going to make a fuss about passports or tickets?'

'Were you sent by the spaceport company?' asked Janie.

'I'm not sure,' said the Doctor. 'I don't think so.'

Janie's face fell. 'Then you haven't come to save us?'

'Oh, well, now, that's a different question altogether,' said the Doctor.

He dropped the book and bounced to his feet. He took Janie's hands and fixed her with his most reassuring stare.

'Because, you see,' said the Doctor, 'saving people, that just happens to be what I do. Can't help myself. So, tell me, Janie – what do you need saving from?'

The duty-free shop had been trashed.

Amy and Rory stood in the doorway, staring at the mess. Shelving units had been knocked over. The tills had been wrenched open and emptied.

'Who could have done this?' asked Amy.

Rory shrugged. 'Maybe we should find a security guard.'

But Amy wanted to explore for herself. She

took a few steps further inside the shop. Her foot crunched on something. She had stepped on a broken perfume bottle.

'Amy, wait,' said Rory, 'do you hear that?'

Amy stood still and listened.

From the back of the shop, she could hear a snuffling sound. Some expensive handbags were piled up on the floor, and Amy realised that the pile was moving.

She felt a chill running down her spine.

There's something in here with us,' she whispered.

'You're different from the other people here, Janie,' said the Doctor.

'Am I?' said Janie.

'Oh, yes,' said the Doctor. 'Look at them. Look at their faces. They're all so gloomy. They need a good... I don't know, a good singalong or something.'

'I don't think that would help,' said Janie.

'Well, maybe not. But you... you chose to come

over here. You spoke to me. These others… If you look, Janie, if you look very carefully out of the corners of your eyes, you can see them. They don't want us to know, but they're watching us.'

'They're as curious as I am,' said Janie. 'They're wondering if you can save them too, but they don't dare ask.'

'Why don't they dare?'

'They're afraid.'

'Afraid of what?' asked the Doctor.

'Afraid to hope,' said Janie.

'Yes, I think I see,' said the Doctor. 'No. Wait. No, I don't see, in fact.'

The young flight attendant sighed. 'We've all been here so long. I was supposed to be working the 2345 flight to Callisto.'

'2345 last night?' asked the Doctor.

Janie looked at him strangely. 'Last year,' she said. 'There's only one flight a year to Callisto, and mine was due out in October 2345. That was five months ago.'

The Doctor looked at Janie. He blinked.

'I'm sorry,' he said. 'I must have misheard you. I thought you said five months.'

'I did,' said Janie.

'But you meant five months as in…?'

'As in five months,' said Janie.

'Let me get this straight,' said the Doctor. 'You've been waiting here, in this spaceport terminal, for a hundred and fifty days now… *in a row?*'

'We've nowhere else to go,' said Janie. 'Terminal 4000 is an interchange station. There's no access from here to any world. The only way out is by ship – and no ships have left since the monsters appeared.'

The Doctor's expression brightened.

'I owe my friends an apology,' he said. 'There is something to see here, after all. Tell me all about these monsters, Janie Collins!'

Amy could see it now.

It was a squat, grey creature, the size and rough shape of a small, fat dog. It was lying in the debris of the duty-free shop. It didn't seem to have noticed her.

'Be careful, Amy,' whispered Rory.

Amy took another step towards the creature. Its nose and ears twitched, and it stood up. It had a stumpy tail and three stubby legs, one at the front and two at the back.

'It's all right,' said Amy. 'It's a dog. Well, a sort of a dog. It looks a bit like a bulldog – y'know, that same little scrunched-up face?'

Rory craned to see from behind her. 'Yeah, I think I saw… there were two or three others like it, out in the departure lounge.'

'There you are, then,' said Amy. 'I bet three-legged alien dogs are this year's must-have pet. This one must be lost, the poor thing.'

'Doesn't mean it won't bite,' said Rory.

But Amy wasn't listening to him. She crouched beside the dog and tickled its chin. 'Hello, boy,' she said. 'What's your name, then?'

The dog looked at Amy for a moment.

Then it roared.

A tentacle shot out from the dog's mouth. It was green and slimy. On the end of the tentacle, there was a second, smaller mouth. This mouth had two tiny rings of sharp teeth, and it was slavering and hissing.

Amy shrieked as the dog-monster leapt at her. Its claws pinned her shoulders to the wall, and the tentacle with the mouth on it darted towards her throat.

CHAPTER 2
WHO LET THE DOGS OUT?

Amy could feel the dog-monster's hot breath on her face.

She fought as hard as she could, her arms flailing about. She caught the creature's chin with her right elbow. Its head snapped to one side. It whimpered. The slimy tentacle in the dog's mouth had just missed Amy's throat.

Amy was still pinned to the wall. She tried to push her attacker away from her. It was too strong. Its claws were digging into her flesh

'Rory,' she yelled, 'do something!'

The Doctor heard an animal roar. It came from

inside the duty-free shop.

An instant later, he heard a shriek.

'Amy!' he cried.

The Doctor began to run. Janie, the flight attendant, grabbed his arm and pulled him back. 'No, Doctor, you can't!'

He brushed her hand away. 'Can't do what?' he snapped. 'Can't go to a friend in need? You'll find I very much can.'

'You can't help her,' said Janie. 'You mustn't even hope you can, or they'll get you too!' She was clinging to the Doctor again.

'Now, that…' he began. He had meant to say something angry, but midway through the sentence he stopped. He frowned in thought. 'That doesn't make any sense at all, actually. Unless…'

The Doctor was missing something.

He closed his eyes and concentrated. He replayed the last few seconds in his mind. He looked for details he hadn't noticed the first time.

His eyes snapped open. 'The dogs!' he exclaimed.

He whirled around. There were two grey, three-legged dogs behind him. The Doctor had seen them before, but hadn't paid them much attention. They had just been mooching about the departure lounge.

They were certainly interested in him, though.

As soon as the Doctor had started towards the duty-free shop, the two dogs had perked up. They had begun to approach him, but cautiously. They were wary of him. They had stopped a short distance away from him.

They watched the Doctor closely.

The Doctor turned to Janie and whispered, 'It's them, isn't it? The dogs. They're your monsters.'

Rory didn't know what to do.

He never knew what to do in situations like this. His every instinct was telling him to run, but he couldn't leave Amy.

He grabbed the first thing to hand. It was a small, round bottle of perfume. He ran at the dog-monster, screaming.

The scream was a sort of war cry, to give Rory confidence. He also hoped it would distract the dog from its victim. It did.

The dog let go of Amy. It dropped back onto all three of its feet. Rory had intended to get right up behind it and hit it with the bottle. As the dog turned his way, however, he lost his nerve. He threw the bottle instead.

He missed the dog. The perfume bottle smashed against the wall. Its liquid green contents exploded across the shop and made everything smell of some alien flower.

The dog growled at Rory. He backed away, holding his hands up. 'There, there,' he said. 'Nice doggie. Good doggie. Sit, Fido, sit. No – stay, Fido, *stay*!'

The dog had tensed as if to spring at Rory.

Instead, it convulsed with what looked like a sneezing fit. Some of the spilled perfume must have got up its nose.

Rory took the opportunity to dash to Amy's side. He took her hand, and they ducked behind one of the few shelving units still standing.

They crept around the edge of the shop, giving the sneezing dog a wide berth. At last, they saw a clear path back to the door.

Amy had been splashed with the perfume too. She wrinkled her nose at the smell. 'Mmm,' she said, 'my new favourite scent. How did you know?'

'Call it husband's intuition,' said Rory.

'You spoil me,' said Amy.

'We *are* still technically on our honeymoon,' said Rory as they hurried out of there.

The passengers in the departure lounge were afraid.

They were edging away from the Doctor, clearing a space around him. Only Janie remained at his side.

The Doctor took out his sonic screwdriver and aimed it at the two dogs in front of him. Janie gasped with delight. 'You have a weapon!'

'I wouldn't call it a weapon exactly,' he confessed. 'More a... tool. A really useful tool, but all the same… okay, a screwdriver. It's a screwdriver.'

Janie's face fell.

'But it's a *sonic* screwdriver,' said the Doctor, 'and that makes it cool, I think.'

The two dogs were circling him, in opposite directions.

Janie shouted at the onlookers: 'Help him, somebody. Can't you help him?'

'The thing about dogs is,' said the Doctor, 'they have brilliant ears. Much better than human ears. They can hear all sorts of things we can't. Of course, these are alien dogs, so their ears might be different. But if I can find a sound frequency they don't like…'

The dogs started growling. They came closer.

The Doctor quickly shut off the sonic screwdriver.

'Ah. Right,' he said. 'Attracting them instead. Best not to do that, then.'

Janie tried again with the passengers. 'The Doctor's here to help us,' she cried. 'He says he can get us out out of here – but he can't if we let the Desponds have him. Don't you think it's time we stood up against them? Don't you think it's time we...'

The two dogs sprang at the Doctor and Janie.

Amy raced out into the departure lounge, leaving Rory behind her, struggling to close an automatic sliding door that was out of power and didn't want to be closed. She cried out for the Doctor, then halted in her tracks, horrified, as she saw him.

The Doctor was being attacked, too. He had grabbed a red, plastic chair and he was using it to fend off another of the alien dog-monsters.

Beside the Doctor, a third dog had knocked a young flight attendant to the ground. She was screaming, but no one made a move to help her.

Rory reappeared at Amy's side.

'Perfume,' said Amy. 'We need more perfume!' Rory groaned as Amy pushed him back towards the duty-free shop.

The door was jammed not quite shut. The gap was too small for Amy to get through –

which meant it was too small for the squat dog-monsters, too.

Rory peered through the glass, looking for the dog he had trapped inside the shop. 'I don't see it,' he said.

The dog sprang out from behind an overturned shelf. It threw itself at the door, but smacked into the glass. Rory started and backed away quickly.

The creature had hurt itself. It staggered away, back into the shop, dazed.

Amy strained at the door. 'If we can budge this an inch,' she said, 'I could wriggle through and grab…'

She realised that Rory wasn't listening to her. He was looking at the Doctor.

They were too late.

The Doctor's attacker had suddenly backed off.

He jabbed his chair in the dog-monster's direction, as a warning. 'Ha!' he shouted.

He had always fancied himself as a lion tamer. Why had he never been a lion tamer, he wondered?

Too cruel to the lion, he supposed.

The dog lay down on its stomach – which was not what the Doctor had expected. It had gone from trying to bite him to ignoring him.

Janie hadn't fared as well. She was on the floor, the other dog standing on her chest. A tentacle had shot out of its mouth and attached itself to Janie's throat.

The Doctor prodded the dog with his chair. 'Shoo,' he said, 'go on, shoo!'

He succeeded in dislodging the creature.

He thought it would have been angry at him. Instead, it just slinked away.

The Doctor crouched beside Janie. She was still awake, but dazed. 'Hmm, you don't appear to be injured,' he said. 'There's a big, red suction mark on your throat, but the skin isn't broken. Weird. You've had a lucky escape, I'd say.'

He helped Janie to her feet, as Amy and Rory ran up. A wary Rory skirted the dog that had attacked the Doctor. It had fallen asleep.

'What did you do to that thing?' asked Amy.

'Why did it back off?'

'Wish I knew,' said the Doctor.

'Does it matter?' asked Janie, with a shrug. She began to walk away.

The Doctor stopped her. 'Whoa,' he said. 'Where do you think you're going?'

'I need a lie down,' said Janie.

'I thought you were going to help us. You were going to tell me about these… dog… things.'

Janie brushed the Doctor's hand off her shoulder. 'What's the point? What can you do? What can anyone do? You should have been here five months ago, Doctor. We needed you then. It's too late now. They've grown too strong!'

The Doctor stared into Janie's eyes. 'You weren't lucky at all, were you? That monster did something to you. No, wait, I'm wrong. It *took something from* you.'

'Of course it did,' snapped Janie. 'Why do you think we call them …?'

'Wait a second,' said the Doctor. 'Oh, oh, oh, I think I'm getting something. Something somebody said.' He slapped himself on the forehead. 'Lion tamers! Did someone mention lion tamers? No? That must just have been me, then.'

The Doctor clicked his fingers. 'I've got it. Desponds!' he whirled around to face Janie again. 'That's what you called them, before they attacked us. Desponds!' the grin faded from his face. 'Which... is what you were just about to say, isn't it?'

'Desponds?' repeated Amy. 'As in "despondent"?'

'Dejected. Down in the mouth. Lacking in hope. And you, Janie Collins, you were so full of hope a few seconds ago, and now... that's what they took from you, isn't it?'

'Doctor, what are you saying?' asked Rory.

'I'm saying these Desponds feed off human emotions, and one emotion in particular,' replied the Doctor. 'They've been preying on the people in this spaceport terminal. They've been sucking the hope right out of them!'

CHAPTER 3

NATURE OF THE BEASTS

The flight attendant, Janie, shuddered at the Doctor's words.

Obviously, he thought, he had guessed right.

An older couple came forward. The woman wrapped a red tartan blanket around Janie's shoulders and murmured comforting words to her.

'Just one more question,' said the Doctor, as the couple led Janie away. They ignored him, so he turned to address the departure lounge in general.

'One question,' he said. 'Just one. How many of these Desponds are there?'

'There are twelve,' the answer came from

behind the Doctor.

He turned to see a black-uniformed man leaning against a wall. He was young and lean, with tightly-curled hair and a thin moustache.

'Twelve,' the Doctor repeated. 'Thanks. And you would be…?'

'Roger. Roger McDowell. I'm with Spaceport Security.'

'Security. Yes. I guessed you might be – what with, you know, the uniform and the yellow badge on your arm that says "Security". I'm observant that way.'

'There were thirteen Desponds,' said Roger, 'but I shot one, once.'

'Well,' said the Doctor, 'good. That's good for you, Roger.' He punched the air in an attempt at a gesture of solidarity. 'Well done.'

The Doctor had always been uncomfortable around guns.

Amy was looking at Janie Collins. The older couple had guided her to a red plastic seat and were fussing over her. They had found her a plastic cup of hot water.

'That could have been me,' said Amy.

Rory reassured her, 'But it wasn't.'

'It gives me goosebumps thinking about it,' said Amy. 'Imagine what it must feel like, to have a part of you just... sucked away.'

The Doctor leaned in between them. 'That's enough moping around,' he said. 'Monsters to deal with. Twelve of them.'

'That's, er, eleven now,' said Rory. 'I trapped a Despond in the duty-free shop.'

The Doctor was already marching away. 'Back door!' he called over his shoulder.

'Oh,' said Rory.

Amy ran after the Doctor. 'What's the plan?'

'Don't know yet,' said the Doctor, 'but it's bound to be good.' He took out the sonic screwdriver, and clicked it a few times. 'I expect there'll be sonicking involved.'

There was.

The Doctor spied a drinks machine. It was

empty. He had Rory help him turn the machine around. He used the sonic screwdriver to unscrew a back panel.

Amy saw another Despond, padding towards the three of them. 'Doctor…' she said.

The Doctor had yanked a handful of circuit boards out of the drinks machine. He had bundled them into Rory's hands. He continued to work as he talked.

'Ah. Okay,' said the Doctor. 'I suggest no one make any sudden moves, and… and try to worry.'

'You mean "try *not* to worry",' said Amy.

'Oh, crikey, no, that would just be reckless!'

'Ah,' said Amy. 'Right. I see… I think. The Desponds feed off hope. They're attracted to it. So, we have to… *not hope* and they should leave us alone.'

'Take your cue from your other half here,' said the Doctor. 'He's a natural born worrier. Right now, he's convinced we're all going to die – isn't that right, Rory?'

'No,' said Rory, defensively. 'That's not what I

think. I was just...' he started, and then realised what he was saying. He looked at the Despond. 'I mean... yes, Doctor,' he said, woodenly. 'We're all going to die. Not the slightest doubt about it.'

'Never mind,' said the Doctor. 'You can work on it. For now, I think the Desponds are more curious than hungry. They've just fed on Janie's hope, after all.'

'One of them did,' said Amy. 'Only one of the Desponds attacked Janie. That still leaves the other eleven.'

'But remember the dog that attacked me,' said the Doctor. 'Remember what it did.'

When the other Despond fed on Janie, yours just gave up.'

'As if it was full up too,' said Rory.

'A psycho-empathic link between the pack!' announced the Doctor. Amy had no idea what that meant, until he explained: 'When one of them feeds, they all feed.'

'And, when one of them gets hungry...' said Rory.

The Despond roared, and out came the slimy tentacle with the second mouth on it.

'Okay,' said Amy, nervously. 'Didn't take too long for dinner to go down…'

The Doctor leapt up. He brushed his two friends aside. He was holding a wire in each hand. The wires trailed back to the drinks machine.

The Despond came galloping at the Doctor. It launched itself at his throat.

The Doctor ducked beneath the monster's feeding tentacle. He thrust the two wires into its stomach. There was a bright flash, a sizzle and a horrible smell of burnt fur.

The Despond hit the floor with a thud. It wasn't seriously hurt, though. It scrambled to its three feet and backed off, whimpering.

Amy noticed that, not far away, a couple more Desponds were looking groggy too. 'I think that electric shock effected all of them,' she said.

'Thought it might,' said the Doctor, 'if only on an emotional level. Should keep them at bay for a while, anyhow.'

Janie came up to the Doctor and his friends. Amy was surprised to see her. Janie's shoulders were still stooped, her eyes downcast.

'I wanted to apologise,' she said. 'I was rude to you back there.'

'Hardly your fault,' said Amy. 'You'd had a pretty nasty shock!'

'If anyone should be sorry,' said Rory, 'it's the Doctor.'

'Er, standing right here,' said the Doctor.

'I just mean,' said Rory, 'you're the one who gave her hope, and that's what attracted the Desponds to her. That's how it works, right?'

Janie pulled up a chair and sat down. 'It was nice, though,' she said, 'to dream about getting out of here, just for a while. I'd forgotten what it was like to dream.'

Janie had been followed, by the older couple who had been helping her.

The woman placed a hand on Janie's shoulder. 'There, there, dear,' she said. She had silver hair and broad shoulders. She wore an orange, floral-patterned dress and clutched a matching handbag to her breast. 'Things aren't so terrible here, are they?'

Her partner was heavy-set, balding, with a grey moustache and steel-rimmed glasses. 'Mrs Henry is right,' he said. 'We have a roof over our heads, and heat and light and water. There are far worse places than this.'

Amy couldn't believe her ears. 'All the same,' she said, 'you must want to go home.'

'What about food?' asked the Doctor. 'You must be running out of food.'

'It's true,' said Mrs Henry, 'we have emptied the food court.'

'And the shops,' the old man added, 'and the dispensing machines.'

'But we've heard a rumour, Mr Henry and I.'

Mr Henry checked over his shoulder for eavesdroppers. 'We have heard there might still be coffee and biscuits in the first-class passenger lounge.'

'And frozen fruit!'

Mr Henry shushed his wife fiercely.

'I'm sorry, dear,' she said, shamefaced. 'I was hoping for too much.'

'You see,' said Janie, 'the Desponds have fed on all of us, some of us many times.'

'They've made us afraid,' said Mrs Henry, 'to hope.'

'And what's the point of hoping, anyway?' asked Mr Henry.

'One of the guards, young Roger, shot a Despond once,' Mrs Henry recalled. 'But he used up all his bullets.'

'We hoped the spaceport company might send someone,' said Janie.

'But we're so far away from any world here,' said Mr Henry.

The Doctor straightened up, and clapped his hands.

'Right,' he said. 'Heard enough. More than enough. A piece of advice, Janie Collins, Mr and Mrs Henry. You might want to steer clear of me

– because, right now, I am the most dangerous person in this room. Ask me why!'

No one asked the Doctor why.

The awkward silence lasted for at least five seconds, before Amy rolled her eyes. 'Why?' she asked.

'Because Rory was right,' said the Doctor. 'The people I call my friends, the ones who really get to know me, there's one thing they can't ever do – and that's give up hope. You see, impossible situations? I get out of four every day before breakfast. Unbeatable odds? I beat them in my spare time. Invincible…'

'We get the point!' said Amy.

'As for last-second saves,' said the Doctor, 'they're my speciality.'

'So, what do we do?' asked Rory.

'We get everyone out of here,' said the Doctor.

'We can't,' said Janie. 'Terminal 4000 has been placed under quarantine.'

'No ships come here any more,' said Mr Henry. 'They haven't for…'

'Five months,' said the Doctor. 'I know. One thing. One teeny-tiny little thing. Well, three things, really.' He marched along the departure lounge. He pointed to three portholes in turn. Or rather, *through* them – to the spaceships behind them.

'Don't you think,' said Janie, 'if escaping was so easy, we'd have done it long ago?'

'Those ships are the ones that brought us all here,' said Mrs Henry.

'They're held by the spaceport's docking clamps,' said Janie. 'They can't be let go until they're cleared for departure. And they can't be cleared until –'

'Until the quarantine is lifted,' guessed Rory.

'Well, then,' said the Doctor. 'Sounds like a plan to me. Lifting the quarantine. Who do we see about that?' He answered his own question. 'No one here from the spaceport company, so the systems must be automated. From where, though? From Space Traffic Control, of course. And that would be…?'

There was another awkward silence.

'No, really, I'm asking,' said the Doctor. 'I don't know.'

'I could show you to the control tower,' said Janie. 'I suppose.'

'Good,' said the Doctor. 'Right away, then, please, before the Desponds decide to feed again.'

'We can keep them away now though, with those wires,' said Amy.

The Doctor shook his head. 'As the Desponds grow hungrier, they'll become more determined. And the three of us – you, Rory and me – we're the only people here they haven't already fed on.'

'We're fresh meat!' Rory realised.

'We'll be like beacons to the Desponds,' said the Doctor. 'We'll be like great big, juicy, hope-filled, packed-with-crunchy-goodness beacons!'

CHAPTER 4
TAKING CONTROL

The Henrys decided to stay in the departure lounge. 'It's what we're used to,' said Mrs Henry. 'Our own two rows of chairs, with our coats and towels to sleep under and the washrooms across the way.'

'And, frankly, after all you said,' said Mr Henry, 'about the danger…'

'We'd just… Mr Henry and I, we'd rather not get our hopes up.'

'I'll leave Rory with you,' said the Doctor, 'in case.'

'In case of what?' protested Rory. The Doctor was already hurrying away from him, after Janie.

'*In case of what?*' Rory shouted after him.

Amy had hung back. She looked at Rory, sympathetically.

'Go on,' said Rory, with a sigh. 'Go after them. It's fine. I'll just… stay here. With the Henrys. And the monsters. *In case.*'

Amy caught up with Janie at the security gate. The Doctor had rushed ahead, but didn't know which way to go. He had to wait for Janie to show him.

Janie glanced at the TARDIS as they passed it, but didn't ask about it. She led the way through the baggage claim hall, around a corner and into a wide concourse.

There were two Desponds here. They had knocked over a queuing system in front of a row of check-in desks. They were playing with the ropes and pillars.

They stopped playing now, however, and turned to watch the newcomers.

To take her mind off the creatures, Amy turned to Janie.

'You know,' she said, 'you surprise me. In a good way, I mean. To be helping us out like this, after what the Desponds… that must be wearing off now, right? You must be feeling a little bit hopeful again, or else why…'

'There is no hope,' said Janie.

Amy eyed the two Desponds. 'No,' she said, pulling a gloomy face. 'No, of course not. No hope.'

'I'm only taking you to Space Traffic Control,' said Janie, 'so you can see that for yourself. Don't make the same mistake we made! You don't want to fight back. The sooner you accept how things must be, the easier it will be for you.'

There was a door in the far wall. Its latch was broken. Janie led the Doctor and Amy through it, and up a spiral staircase. It opened out into a round room with portholes all around it, looking out into space.

'Here it is,' said Janie. 'The control tower. Do you see what I mean now?'

Amy looked around Space Traffic Control in dismay.

She saw exactly what Janie had meant.

Rory sat on a red plastic chair, glaring at a Despond. It was mooching around, a little too close to his feet for comfort.

Something of a buzz had gone up around the departure lounge. A knot of people had formed by the *bureau de change*, and were talking in low voices. Mr Henry had gone over to see what they were saying. He returned with news.

'There's a raid planned,' he whispered, 'on the first-class lounge.'

Mrs Henry clapped her hands together. 'Oh, how wonderful!'

'A raid?' said Rory. 'But why? What for?'

Mr Henry glared at him. 'For the coffee, of course. And the biscuits.'

'It really is unfair,' said Mrs Henry. 'We're so hungry out here, there's hardly any food left, but in there... Who is in there these days, Mr Henry? I forget.'

'It must be Captain Stone's group,' said Mr

Henry. 'I haven't seen them around in a while. Yes, I'm sure that's right. They won the last raid, remember?'

'I can't believe I'm hearing this,' said Rory. 'Listen to yourselves. Haven't you got enough to worry about without fighting each other?'

Rory saw Mr Henry's warning glare. He looked over his shoulder.

The Despond he had been watching was ambling towards him.

'He'll understand, dear,' said Mrs Henry to her husband. 'Once he's been here as long as we have. Once the Desponds have fed on him two or three times.'

The Despond was still approaching, now with more purpose.

Rory leapt to his feet. He addressed the Despond as firmly as he could. 'No,' he said, 'you don't want to feed on me. I… I'd probably give you indigestion.'

Mr Henry shook his head. 'The classic mistake,' he said.

'I know, dear,' his wife sighed. 'Hoping they won't attack him.'

'And, of course, that hope attracts them all the more.'

'I'm a pessimist,' insisted Rory. 'Ask the wife. Ask Amy. If it wasn't for her… she's the only reason I'm travelling with the Doctor. Last-second saves? Really? He's let me die, more than once. Long story. I'm just saying.'

He was backing away slowly, towards the gutted drinks machine with its trailing wires. He was hoping to…

No, Rory told himself sternly. *Don't hope!*

Too late. Another Despond had appeared, behind him. It was cutting him off from the drinks machine.

Rory picked up a chair. It was no use, though. He knew he couldn't fend off two of the creatures at once.

'I imagine this is why the Doctor left you with us, dear,' said Mrs Henry.

'Yes,' said Mr Henry. 'He knew you could lead

the Desponds away from us.'

The creatures were almost upon Rory now. He threw the chair at the nearest of them and ran for it. The two Desponds came barrelling after him.

'What happened here?' cried the Doctor.

'Well, obviously,' said Janie, 'other people had the same idea as you.'

The Doctor massaged his temples as if he had a headache. 'No, not the same,' he moaned. 'Not the same idea at all. I wasn't planning on wanton vandalism!'

There were instrument banks all the way around the room. They had been wrenched open, wires pulled out of them. Monitor screens had been put through, indicator lights smashed. It reminded Amy of the damage to the duty-free shop.

'We came here months ago,' said Janie. 'We tried to get the computers to release the docking clamps on the passenger ships.'

'By smashing everything to pieces?' said Amy. 'Good plan!'

'We couldn't find the security codes,' said Janie. 'People got frustrated.'

The Doctor had already slid under one of the consoles. He was using the sonic screwdriver to repair some broken wires.

'Didn't you hear me?' said Janie. 'Even if you could fix the controls…'

'The Doctor can fix them,' said Amy.

'Even if he does,' said Janie, 'we don't have the codes to access the computers.'

'One problem at a time,' came the Doctor's muffled voice from beneath the console. 'Amy, keep an eye on the stairs. Let me know if any Desponds…'

He broke off in mid-sentence as, suddenly, there was a pop and an electric flash.

'Doctor,' cried Amy, 'are you okay? What happened?'

She heard a rumbling sound behind her. She whirled around. A security door had just slammed down over the exit.

The Doctor sat up and blew ruefully on his

fingers. 'I think I may just have reactivated a system I shouldn't have reactivated.'

Janie sank into a chair. 'I knew something like this would happen,' she moaned.

'Doctor,' said Amy, 'can you hear that sound? A sort of hissing?'

The Doctor's face lengthened. 'Ah.'

'"Ah" what?' said Amy. 'What does "ah" mean? "Ah" doesn't sound good.'

'I think…' said the Doctor. 'Now, Amy, don't panic, but I think I may just have triggered a security lockdown. And, in fact, I think…'

Janie doubled up, coughing. Amy's throat was itching too, and her eyes were beginning to water.

'You see,' said the Doctor, 'the main computer has detected an unclassified alien life form in this room – which would be me – and so, it's…'

'It's disinfecting the control tower!' gasped Amy. She barely got the words out before she too had a coughing fit. She could hardly breathe.

Amy could see a metal grille in the wall, near the floor. The hissing was coming from down there. *It's pumping gas into the room*, she realised. *Invisible poison gas!*

And Amy, the Doctor and Janie were all trapped in here.

The Doctor stood up and aimed his sonic screwdriver at the security door.

The sonic screwdriver whined and glowed a fierce shade of green, but nothing else happened. The door stayed closed. The Doctor groaned. 'Deadlock sealed!' he said.

Amy had an idea. She shrugged off her baggy jumper, and dropped down by the grille in the wall. She stuffed her jumper into the grille, to block it up.

'Nice thinking,' said the Doctor. 'Should slow down the inflow of gas, at least. Otherwise? Try breathing through a hanky, if you have one. Oh, and stand on a chair.'

'What?'

'The gas is heavier than air,' said the Doctor. 'It's filling the room from the bottom.'

'Right,' said Amy.

She didn't have a handkerchief, but Janie had two moist towelettes. Amy took one, gratefully, and pressed it over her nose and mouth. She climbed up onto a chair and pulled Janie up after her. It didn't seem to help much.

Amy felt as if tiny claws were tearing at her throat. There were hot tears streaming down her cheeks. 'What about you, Doctor?' she croaked.

The Doctor shrugged. 'Doesn't seem to affect me,' he said. 'There's no reason why it should, of course. A Time Lord's physiology is very different to…'

'Great,' said Amy. 'I mean, that's really great for you, considering the whole point of this is to – what was it again? Oh, yes – kill the alien life form!'

The Doctor grinned. 'Ironic, isn't it?'

Then, he became serious. 'Of course, that's how we fix this,' he said. 'That's how we get the lockdown lifted.'

'How?' asked Amy.

'Obvious, isn't it?' said the Doctor. 'We give the

computer what it wants.'

'But… but doesn't it want…?'

'The computer wants me dead,' said the Doctor. 'So, to get you and Janie out of this room, it looks like I'll have to die.'

CHAPTER 5
THE DOCTOR DIES

Rory pelted across the departure lounge, a Despond snapping at his heels. *It's going to catch me,* he thought, *I know it is! Where's the Doctor when I need him?*

The creature fastened its teeth around Rory's trouser cuff. It tugged, and he lost his balance and fell over.

Rory's hands and knees slipped on the floor tiles, as the Despond dragged him backwards. He went on the offensive. He bopped the Despond on its scrunched-up nose. It recoiled and Rory scrambled to his feet.

The other Despond was charging at him, its

feeding tentacle extended.

He ducked behind a young woman in a fur coat. She shrieked as she saw the two Desponds coming at her. 'I'm sorry,' said Rory, mortified. 'I didn't mean…'

Of course, the woman was in no danger. It was Rory the Desponds wanted; anyone else was just in their way.

He gained a little ground on them, as they dodged around the shrieking woman. He knew it wouldn't last, though. The Desponds were faster than he was.

Rory heard a voice calling, 'Over here!'

It was Roger, the security guard he had met before. He was standing in the doorway of the men's washroom, beckoning to Rory urgently.

Rory had no better ideas.

He ran into the washroom. The Desponds were right behind him. Rory slammed the door in their faces. He fell back against it, breathlessly. He could hear the Desponds scratching at the other side of the door, and one of them howled.

Rory turned to Roger, to thank him for his help.

He froze as he saw that Roger was holding a gun on him.

'Doctor, what… what are you saying? What…?

Amy couldn't speak any more. She had swallowed too much of the poison gas. Her lungs felt as if they were on fire.

'No time to discuss it,' said the Doctor. 'I need you to trust me and to do as I say.'

Amy nodded helplessly.

'In a moment, Amy,' said the Doctor, 'that security door is going to open. As soon as it does, get out of here. Take Janie. Don't worry about me.'

Amy could hardly see. The gas had made her eyes swell up.

She could just make out the shape of the Doctor, sitting in a chair. His chin was resting on his chest. He looked like he was going to sleep.

Amy wanted to scream at him: *'How can I not worry about you? After what you said, about you having to die…'* But she was overcome by another coughing fit.

Janie had passed out. She was leaning on Amy's shoulder.

Amy was growing light-headed too. Her legs felt weak. She tried to hold her breath, but she was coughing too much. She couldn't take much more of this.

To her relief, the security door rose.

Amy lifted Janie down from the chair on which they both stood. She dragged her across the room and out through the doorway.

She collapsed on the stairs outside. Fresh air had never tasted so sweet to her. Amy gulped it down by the lungful, feeling stronger with each breath she took.

She remembered the Doctor. He was still inside the control room.

She looked back and saw him. The Doctor was still slumped in his chair. He wasn't moving. Amy couldn't tell, from here, if he was breathing or not.

The Doctor had told her not to worry about him. Easier said than done!

Amy had to go back for him.

Before she could, the security door slammed down again in front of her nose.

Amy cried out, 'No!' She hammered on the closed door with her fists.

'Doctor,' she yelled, 'what have you done? Doctor!'

On the other side of the door, the Doctor opened his eyes and grinned. He was very impressed with himself.

His plan had been simple. He had put himself into a trance. A deep trance. So deep that his heartbeats and breathing had been almost undetectable.

He had tricked the main computer into thinking he was dead.

So, of course, it had ended the lockdown. It had opened the security door, and let Amy and Janie go.

Now, the Doctor had come round and the computer had sealed off Space Traffic Control again. It was pumping more poison gas into the room.

That was okay, though – because the gas didn't affect the Doctor. And, although he was still trapped, he was right where he needed to be.

The Doctor flexed his long fingers. It was time to get to work.

'Um,' said Rory. 'Okay. So, obviously, you have a gun.'

'I'm sorry,' said Roger.

'You're sorry. That's good. Well, that's a start. So, why *are* you…? I mean, if you don't mind my asking. I don't mean to pressure you or anything, but…'

'We need your help,' said Roger.

Rory was relieved. At least Roger wasn't planning to shoot him. Anyway, he had just remembered something he had heard.

'I see. Right,' he said. 'And you thought the best way to ask me was at gunpoint?'

He advanced on Roger, holding out his hand. 'Why not give me the gun, and then we can… I don't know… talk, I suppose.'

Roger backed away from him. 'Don't come any closer,' he said, 'or I'll shoot.'

'I don't think you will,' said Rory. He was gaining in confidence.

'I mean it,' said Roger. 'I shot a Despond once. I killed it.'

'And you used up all your bullets. Mrs Henry told us so.'

Roger turned quite pale. His aim wavered. Obviously, Rory was right. He smiled as he reached for the security guard's gun again.

Roger struck like lightning. He turned the gun around, and smacked Rory in the temple with the butt end of it. Lights exploded behind Rory's eyes. He felt his legs turning to jelly. He saw the tiles on the washroom floor rushing up to meet him.

It wasn't fair, he thought, as he lost consciousness. He had just been getting the hang of being a hero!

Amy had given up hammering on the security door. She was getting no answer. It was probably soundproof, she thought. At least, she hoped that was the reason.

Janie came up behind her. She laid a comforting hand on Amy's shoulder. 'Don't worry,' said Janie. 'I'm sure the Doctor will be fine.'

Amy looked at Janie, surprised. She was recovering from the Despond's attack, then. She was beginning to hope again. *Well, if she can do it,* thought Amy, *so can I.*

'You're right,' she said. 'I've seen the Doctor stand up to Daleks and Weeping Angels. He's alive in there, I know he is, and he's working on a way to help us.'

'So, what do we do?' asked Janie.

Amy shrugged. 'I don't know,' she said. 'Find Rory, I suppose.'

The mood in the departure lounge had changed. Amy sensed it as soon as she and Janie walked in. The stranded passengers in the lounge were no longer without purpose. They had formed into groups. They were whispering to each other, plotting. Some of them had armed themselves, with chairs or sticks or bottles from the duty-free shop.

'I know this feeling,' said Amy. 'This is like a… a rowdy party, when things are about to turn ugly. The Desponds can feel it too. Look.'

They could see five Desponds among the crowd. The dog-like creatures were awake, and very much alert.

'They do this,' said Janie, before correcting herself. '*We* do this, every few weeks – more often, since the food has been running out. It's… I don't know, I suppose it's a way of releasing the frustration we all feel. They're… we're going to war.'

One of the larger groups had just made its move.

At one end of the departure lounge, there was a marble water feature. In an alcove next to this, there was an unobtrusive doorway. It had been boarded up with planks from the inside.

'That's the first-class passenger lounge,' said Janie.

A score or so of people were marching towards that doorway.

One of them, a man with a stubbly beard, had a fire extinguisher in his hands. He rammed it into the wooden boards. Amy saw hands reaching through the planks from the other side, trying to push the bearded man away. But the other members of his group were straining forward too, lending their shoulders to the effort.

'Come on,' said Janie, 'let's get out of here.'

'Wait,' said Amy, 'what about Rory? I don't see Rory. He was with the Henrys. Can you see the Henrys?'

'*Smash it all down!*'

A teenager in a combat jacket had leapt up onto a chair. He was punching the air as he yelled, 'Smash down the class barriers. No first class or business class or club class. An end to privilege. Free coffee and biscuits for all!'

A Despond leapt at him. It knocked him off his chair, and fed on him. It was over before Amy could do anything.

The Despond waddled away, full. The teenager stayed where he was, on the floor. He rolled onto his side and pulled his knees up to his chest, miserably.

Apart from Amy and Janie, no one seemed to notice. The passengers were all too busy getting angry, surging towards the boarded-up doorway.

Amy was still looking for Rory. Instead, she saw something odd. She saw the security guard, Roger, pushing a luggage trolley across the departure lounge, far from the action. Whatever was on that trolley, it was covered by a blanket.

Amy didn't have time to think about it.

She heard a terrible splintering sound. The planks across the doorway had been broken. The way into the first-class lounge was now clear.

The passengers had started to fight with each other, each in their little groups, each group determined to beat the others through that doorway.

And Amy and Janie were caught right in the middle of the chaos.

CHAPTER 6
TURBULENCE

Amy kept her head down as sticks were waved and punches thrown around her.

We've got to get out of here, she thought, *before someone gets hurt!* She grabbed hold of Janie's hand and tried to pull her to safety.

To her dismay, their path was blocked by a huge, angry-looking woman with some kind of a baton. It took Amy a second to recognise it as a metal detector wand.

She squared up to the huge woman, putting on her no-nonsense face. 'Now, look here, um, madam,' Amy snarled, 'we don't want to have to fight you. So, why don't you just step of our way and we'll –'

Janie grabbed a luggage trolley and rammed it into the huge woman's shins. The woman whimpered with pain and dropped her weapon.

'Okay,' said Amy. 'That works too.' They ran past the huge woman, but found a Despond in front of them. It growled at them.

Janie squealed and ran away from the Despond – right back into the thick of the fighting. Amy was forced to follow her.

The Doctor had lashed a few more wires together. He stood up and flicked some switches on an instrument panel.

All around the Space Traffic Control room, monitor screens and indicator lights – those that hadn't been smashed – began to light up.

'Now,' said the Doctor to himself, 'to get those docking clamps released.'

His attention was drawn to a bank of twelve screens. Seven of them were broken, but the other five were showing scenes from around the spaceport. Security camera feeds.

The Doctor saw what looked like a riot in progress, in the departure lounge.

He ran his fingers through his hair in exasperation. 'What are they doing down there?' he wailed.

He only hoped his friends weren't involved. They wouldn't be, the Doctor told himself. Amy and Rory were too sensible for that.

Then, on a cracked screen, he saw a wave of red hair. Amy. She was right in the centre of things, with Janie. *Of course she is!* thought the Doctor.

It looked like Amy and Janie were about to get trampled. They needed help. But what could the Doctor do? The security door was still down.

He couldn't leave this room.

'Amy, help me!' shrieked Janie. 'I can't get up!'

Janie had fallen over. The heaving crowd had closed in around her – and, whenever she tried to stand, she was knocked down again.

'Take my hand!' Amy urged her. She was being pushed and prodded too, but she was determined to stand her ground.

Amy stooped to help Janie up – and came face to face with a Despond.

She froze. She stared at the Despond. The Despond stared back at Amy. It opened its mouth, to display its feeding tentacle.

Amy forced herself to close her eyes. She thought very hard. *There is no hope*, she told herself – and she tried to make herself believe it. *'The Doctor's trapped in Space Traffic Control, I don't know if he's alive or dead, Rory's disappeared and everyone's fighting and the Desponds are everywhere and...'*

She felt a genuine pang of despair. Perhaps there *was* no hope, she thought.

Then Amy heard a cry. She opened her eyes. The Despond had turned away from her. It had clamped its mouth around the leg of a middle-aged man. He was trying to kick the Despond away – but now, a second creature bounded to the aid of the first.

The two Desponds dragged the man to the

floor. One pinned him down with its claws, while the other went for his throat with its feeding tentacle.

Amy had kept the Desponds from attacking her – so, instead, they had found another victim. She felt responsible.

'*Psst!*'

A figure beckoned to Amy, from beside the water feature at the end of the departure lounge. It was Mrs Henry. 'Over here, dear,' she called in a loud whisper.

The fighting had shifted away from Amy, as the passengers avoided the feeding Desponds. Janie had managed to get to her feet. She tugged at Amy's arm.

'There's nothing you can do for him,' said Janie. She must have guessed what Amy was thinking.

'But it's my fault he's –' began Amy.

'No,' said Janie. 'This is what happens. This is what always happens. We think we're safe, because we aren't hoping for much. We aren't hoping for escape or anything like that, just a few little luxuries. But it gets out of hand. We get caught up in the moment. We hope too much – and that's when people get hurt.'

The Desponds had finished feeding now, anyway. It was too late.

'Better him than us,' said Janie.

She led the way to where Mrs Henry was waiting.

The Doctor sniffed the air. The smell of the poison gas had lessened.

'Well, that had to happen,' he said. 'Your tanks have run dry. So, now what?'

He was addressing the computer that ran Space Traffic Control.

'I know you can hear me,' said the Doctor. 'You're configured for voice activation. This is your alien infestation here – or the Doctor, to my friends.'

Letters streamed across a tiny read-out screen:

"Alien infestation detected. Lockdown in force."

'Oh, come now,' said the Doctor, 'I know you can do better than that.'

The same message scrolled across the screen again.

'Think about it,' said the Doctor. 'Well, not "think", I know you can't think exactly, but run this through your processors. You work on logical principles, right? So, tell me, what is the logic of keeping me in this room? I'm waiting.'

"Alien infestation contained," the read-out said.

'Right. Yes,' said the Doctor. 'I get that. You've contained me. But why?'

"Awaiting instructions."

'No, sorry. Won't wash. There's no one here from the spaceport company. You'll have to follow your existing programming. Your sensors detect an alien life form in this room. So, you trap it in here, yes?'

"Thesis is correct."

'And you kill it. And that's the important part, the killing, because this is Space Traffic Control. It's okay for unclassified life forms to wander about the rest of the terminal – but as soon as one of them gets in here, it has to die.'

"Thesis is correct."

'And of course, you don't distinguish between good life forms and bad life forms. No, don't even try to answer that. There's just one little fly in your ointment: me. I'm not that easy to kill. You might have noticed.'

"Thesis is..."

'Yes, yes, yes, "thesis is correct". Don't interrupt me when I'm speaking. You see, your programming has failed. You can see that, can't you? You've confined your alien infestation – me – to the last place you want me to be.'

"Awaiting instructions," said the read-out screen.

'You don't have time to wait,' said the Doctor.

"Awaiting instructions."

'And you don't need new instructions. You just need to apply your logic. You have an alien infestation in here, one you can't seem to kill. For as long as you keep this control room in lockdown, that can't change. But open the security door, and maybe – just maybe – the infestation will leave of its own accord.'

The Doctor waited.

The computer didn't answer him.

He sighed. 'I'm sure this used to be much easier. Okay, I'll leave you to ponder on that for a moment. In the meantime, I'll see what I can do from in here.'

The Doctor walked up to an instrument panel. He flicked a switch.

Bang! An electrical charge jolted through the Doctor's body. He was hurled back across the room, into the wall. He slid to the floor and lay there for a second, his eyes closed.

His eyes snapped open.

'So, it's like that, is it?' said the Doctor. 'All right, then. This means war!'

'We're so pleased you decided to join us, dears,' said Mrs Henry.

She was standing with her husband, and a group

of six or seven older passengers. Like the others, they had armed themselves as best they could. Mr Henry had a walking stick, which he waved about vigorously. He almost hit Amy with it.

'Indeed,' said Mr Henry. 'You're precisely what our little group needs: two pairs of younger, fitter hands to fight with us.'

'Now, hang on a minute,' said Amy. 'That's not what we…'

'We're biding our time, you see,' said Mrs Henry.

'We're waiting for the others to tire themselves out,' said Mr Henry.

'And then we'll swoop! It was Mr Henry's idea.'

'That first-class lounge will be ours tonight, you mark my words.'

'We'll have coffee and chocolate biscuits and, oh, flowers and moist towelettes.'

'We're just looking for Rory,' said Amy. 'My husband. He was with you.'

'We haven't seen him, dear,' said Mrs Henry, 'have we, Mr Henry?'

Mr Henry shook his head. 'Not for some time.

Some protector he turned out to be.'

'You must have seen where he went!' said Amy, frustrated.

'I don't think so, dear,' said Mrs Henry. 'Unless…'

'Unless?'

A shifty look crept over Mrs Henry's face. 'Unless Captain Stone took him. Captain Stone and his group. They're in the first-class lounge, you see. They…'

'Uh-huh,' said Amy. 'I think I do see, yeah.'

A group of passengers had forced their way into the first-class lounge. Another group had gone in after them, intent on dragging them back out again.

'And this happens every few weeks, you said?' said Amy to Janie.

'That's right,' said Janie.

Amy nodded. *Makes sense*, she thought. *The first-class lounge is probably in the same state as the duty-free shop. And the Space Traffic Control tower. And most of the rest of the spaceport, by now.*

'So,' said Mrs Henry eagerly, to Amy, 'will you

help us to take the first-class lounge or not? You never know, your husband could be in there.'

The problem was, thought Amy, Mrs Henry was right.

No one knew where Rory had got to. If he wasn't in the first-class passenger lounge, then where else could he be?

CHAPTER 7
ENGINE FAILURE

Rory opened his eyes. It was dark. His head ached. He was lying on his back, on a hard surface, under a thick blanket. The blanket irritated Rory's nose. He sneezed.

The blanket was whipped away. Rory saw the security guard, Roger, standing over him. A memory came rushing back to him.

'Did you… did you just knock me out?' asked Rory, blearily.

He tried to sit up. To his surprise, Roger stooped to help him.

'It was the only way to get you here,' said Roger.

Rory was on a luggage trolley. It was jammed

into an aisle between two columns of fixed seats in a long, narrow, compartment.

There were folded-up tables on the back of each seat, with cup holders.

Roger pulled an oxygen mask down from the ceiling. He handed it to Rory. 'Here,' he said, 'use this. It'll help to bring you round.'

They were on a spaceship, Rory realised. A passenger spaceship.

The fighting had spread all across the departure lounge. The Desponds were having a field day, claiming victim after victim.

Amy was waiting, along with Janie, the Henrys and their group , in the corner by the water feature. Someone had given her a plank to use as a weapon. It looked to Amy like a broken shelf from the duty-free shop.

Most of the passengers had forgotten what they were fighting about. They were lashing out blindly, caught up in the moment, giving vent to their pent-up emotions.

The way into the first-class lounge had been left clear.

Mr Henry raised his walking stick above his head. '*To battle!*' he yelled.

His group surged forward, following his lead. Only Janie stayed behind.

Amy was swept along with the others. She didn't want to be here. She didn't want to have to fight. But what about Rory, she thought? What if he was in trouble, inside that room, and he needed her?

'*Have you asked him yet?*'

Rory looked up. A newcomer had just entered the passenger compartment, through an airlock at its rear. He was wearing a bulky white spacesuit with a helmet.

'I was about to,' said Roger.

'About to ask me what?' asked Rory. 'Look, where are we, anyway?'

'*You're aboard my ship,*' said the man in the spacesuit. His voice came out through a speaker in his chest unit.

Rory looked at Roger. 'We aren't…? I mean, we haven't left the spaceport?'

Roger shook his head. 'We can't ship out until the computers release the…'

'The docking clamps. I know.' Rory breathed out, relieved.

'You see, Cap? He knows his stuff.'

The newcomer lifted off his helmet, so Rory could see his face. He was probably in his mid-fifties. He was short, with leathery skin and deep frown lines around his eyes.

'Cap runs a space charter service,' said Roger. 'At least, he used to run one, until he got stuck here at Terminal 4000 with the rest of us.'

'Okay,' said Rory.

'But that's about to change. Cap and me, we've a plan for getting out of here.'

'Good,' said Rory. 'That's great. I'm sorry – can we fast-forward to the part I still don't understand? That's the part where you beat me unconscious.'

It was the other man – Cap – who answered him. 'Thing is, son,' he drawled, 'I lost my tech guy in a fire fight with the Sidewinder Syndicate a few months back.'

'So, we need a replacement.'

Rory stared at Roger. He wasn't sure if he had heard him right.

Cap was peeling off the rest of his spacesuit. 'I've tuned up my old engines till they sing,' he said. 'A little more juice through the couplings, and I figure we'll be there.'

'I still say we could do it,' said Roger, 'with the new fuel mix I suggested.'

'Not worth the risk, son,' said Cap. 'Not now we have the expert here.'

'Expert?' repeated Rory. He blinked. 'You don't mean... *me?*'

A new sound rang out through the departure lounge: three melodic chimes, followed by a short burst of speaker static. Then, a voice: 'Ladies and gentlemen, your attention please.'

Mr Henry came to a halt. The rest of his group faltered too, behind him. Mr Henry lowered his walking stick, and raised his head to listen.

'Orion Spaceways Flight Number 47, departing to Drahva, now boarding at Gate 14 and a half. This is a final call for Orion Spaceways Flight Number 47. To Drahva.'

Amy could hardly believe her ears. She recognised that voice.

It belonged to the Doctor.

The Doctor was still in the Space Traffic Control room. He was watching the departure lounge on the security camera screens.

The passengers had stopped fighting. It was as if they had come out of a collective trance. They were looking at each other, and up at the ceiling, confused.

Time for another announcement, thought the Doctor.

He operated the tannoy, very carefully. He had stripped the insulation from an electric cable and wrapped it around his hand, so he wouldn't get another shock.

'All right,' he addressed the departure lounge,

'that was a lie. You probably noticed, there is no Gate 14 and a half. And who'd want to go to Drahva, anyway? All those... Drahvins. I just wanted to make you all stop and think for a second.'

The passengers were breaking up. They were picking up their red plastic seats, which had been scattered in the riot. They were sitting down, dispirited.

'Which... okay, you appear to have done now,' said the Doctor. 'You've stopped... hitting each other with sticks. Well done. So, I'll just shut up, then.'

The Doctor shut off the tannoy with a scowl. He didn't like what he had just had to do. His plan had worked, though. The Desponds – so excited a moment ago – were slinking away to digest their recent feast. The Doctor had saved the passengers from them – by raising their hopes and then crushing them again.

He switched the tannoy back on. 'I'm so sorry,' he said.

On one of the camera screens, he saw Amy.

She looked bedraggled. She had located the camera and was miming something at it. She was asking the Doctor how he was.

'Amy, hold on,' the Doctor broadcast. 'I'm coming down there.'

He stepped away from the controls. He addressed the Space Traffic Control computer. 'Yes, you heard that right,' he said. 'I'm going out there, and I expect you'll probably try to stop me. So. Are you ready for Round Two?'

"Alien infestation detected," said the read-out screen. **"Lockdown in force."**

The Doctor smiled grimly. 'That's exactly what I thought you'd say.'

'I keep telling you,' insisted Rory, 'I'm a nurse! I don't know the first thing about…'

'I saw you in the terminal.' Roger had pulled his gun again. 'I saw how you and your friend rewired that drinks machine.'

'Not me and my friend. Just him. Just the Doctor. I was just… he put some circuit boards in my hands, and I... look, why don't we go and find him? I'm sure he...'

'Roger,' growled Cap. 'You promised me an engineer!'

'He's lying,' said Roger. He rounded on Rory. 'You're lying! You can't be a nurse! They wouldn't have sent you here if you couldn't...'

'I wasn't sent here!'

'I didn't go to all this trouble for nothing,' snapped Roger. 'You're going to fix up those engines, or...' He looked down at his gun. His empty gun.

Roger swallowed. 'Look,' he pleaded. 'We're so close to getting out of here. We'll take you with us if you help us. It'll just be the three of us.'

'The three of...?' Rory looked around the empty passenger compartment. 'You could fit about fifty people in here. Four trips, and you'd have the whole of the spaceport evacuated. Why don't you...?'

Cap shook his head firmly. 'That's a bad idea, son.'

'You've seen what they're like in there,' said

Roger, 'the passengers. They've been fed on by the Desponds one too many times. They've no hope left.'

'And you do?' said Rory.

'The Desponds can't get to us in here,' said Roger.

'I haven't stepped outside this ship in two months,' said Cap, proudly.

'I've been out to fetch supplies,' said Roger, 'but only when the Desponds aren't on the prowl, when it's safe. That's how we've been able to start hoping again.'

'We open that airlock door to all-comers, and what do you think'll happen? We'll have them damn dogs in here faster'n you can say Jack Robinson.'

'We can't take that risk,' said Roger.

'It's a shame about those other guys,' said Cap, 'but, hey, we'll be doing them a mercy. They're all out of food in there, anyway.'

'What do you mean, "anyway"?' asked Rory.

Roger stared at the floor. He shuffled his feet. 'Well, Cap thinks…' he mumbled.

'If we can get that extra juice to the engines,' said Cap, 'we can tear this ship free of the docking clamps.'

'It's just,' said Roger, 'there's a chance that we'll, um, you know… tear a hole in the side of the spaceport too.'

Cap shrugged. 'Like I said, the folks in there, they're all gonna die anyway.'

'You're mad!' cried Rory.

Cap's eyes gleamed fiercely. 'Maybe we are,' he snapped. 'Maybe that's what it does to a man, being stuck in the armpit of the universe for five long months.'

'But you're going to help us,' said Roger quietly, 'or we'll…'

'Or you won't like the consequences!' Cap snarled. He had bundled up his spacesuit into a giant ball. He thrust it into Rory's arms.

Rory looked at the spacesuit. He looked at his two captors.

Of course, he thought, with an inward groan. The engines must be on the outside of the ship.

He was supposed to put on this suit… and walk out into space!

'This day just keeps getting better and better,' Rory muttered.

CHAPTER 8
THE DESPONDS FEED

'Where are you going?' asked Janie.

Amy halted in her tracks. She turned back to the young flight attendant. 'You heard the Doctor,' she said. 'He's alive. He's on his way down here.'

'So what?'

'So, I'm going to meet him. He's probably worked out a way to save us all by now, and...' Amy's voice trailed off.

Janie was staring past her, afraid. Amy turned around slowly.

There was a Despond right behind her.

Amy could have kicked herself. The sound of

the Doctor's voice had made her hope again. She hadn't been able to help it.

'It's all right,' said Janie, relaxing. 'Look at it.'

'I'm looking,' said Amy. 'Looking right at the monster.'

'It's curious about you,' said Janie, 'but it doesn't want to feed. The Desponds must have overeaten in the riot.'

'So, what, they've all got bellyache?'

'I wouldn't count on it lasting,' said Janie.

'But while it does, we're safe. We're safe to hope. In which case... Janie, come with me. Come and meet the Doctor with me. We can –'

'No,' said Janie. 'I've been fed on once already today. I'll just stay here. With Mr and Mrs Henry and the others. I think that's best.'

'I understand,' said Amy.

'Watch this,' said the Doctor. 'It's going to be good.'

He grabbed an office chair and rolled it on its castors to the edge of the round room. He stepped up onto its seat.

Now, he could reach a camera, which was hanging from the ceiling.

The Doctor gripped the camera, with his hand still wrapped in the cable insulation. He wrenched the camera from its bracket and hopped down from the chair.

'Now,' he said, 'unless I've very much missed my guess…'

He inspected the device. 'Oh, yes. A body scanner. X-rays, thermal imaging, the works. Nice. Ideal for detecting, say, unclassified life forms in your control room.'

He looked at the computer read-out screen. It was blank.

'Go on,' said the Doctor. 'Try running a scan now. See what it says.'

Nothing happened for a moment, as if the computer was reluctant to follow the instruction. Then, the words appeared: **"No alien infestation detected."**

'Of course not,' said the Doctor. 'How could there be? I've disconnected your scanner. But that doesn't mean a thing to you, does it? You have your programming. The only thing you care about is…' He pointed to the read-out screen.

"No alien infestation detected."

'And that means…?'

"Lockdown lifted."

'Good old computer logic!' crowed the Doctor. 'Gotta love it!'

The heavy security door rumbled back up into the ceiling. The Doctor stepped outside, and onto the spiral staircase that led back down to the main concourse.

He was four steps down when a thought occurred to him.

'Oh, oh, oh!' cried the Doctor. He whirled around, aiming the sonic screwdriver.

A chair came careering across the control room towards him. At the same time, the computer tried to close the security door again.

The chair was jammed beneath the security door. There was now a low gap, to each side of the chair, through which a person could crawl.

'Nice try,' said the Doctor. 'You're good. But I'm better.'

Cap's spacesuit was a tight fit on the much taller Rory. Rory struggled to get his shoulders into it, and was disappointed when he succeeded.

Cap lowered the helmet over Rory's head. He fastened the seals on it. Then, he hefted an air tank onto Rory's back.

Next, Cap attached a flexible tube from the tank to Rory's chest unit. Rory felt a little light-headed as his helmet filled up with oxygen.

He was still terrified about going out into space, even with all this protection. But he didn't know what else he could do, at least for now.

Roger had disappeared into the cockpit of the spaceship. He returned now – wearing another spacesuit. *You didn't think I'd let you go out there alone?* His sneering voice sounded inside Rory's helmet, through a radio link.

'Roger here'll be making sure you don't get up to any tricks,' Cap drawled.

'Like what?' asked Rory, sullenly.

'*Like sabotaging the engines instead of fixing them,*' said Roger.

'I wouldn't know how to do either. As I keep trying to tell you…'

'You'll be connected to this ship,' said Cap, 'by a single lifeline. One word from Roger, over the radio, and…' Cap made a slashing motion with his hand.

'*That lifeline gets cut,*' said Roger. '*You'll be cast adrift. In space.*'

'Perfect,' muttered Rory.

Cap led the way to the airlock at the back of the ship. He picked up a tool kit, which he handed to Rory. It was heavier than it looked. Its weight almost pulled Rory over.

'You ready for this, son?' asked Cap.

'No,' said Rory.

'Too bad,' said Cap. He wrenched open the airlock door.

Amy met the Doctor in front of the TARDIS. She

leapt at him and enveloped him in a tight hug. She knew it would embarrass him, but right now she didn't care.

'Did you do it?' asked Amy. 'Did you end the quarantine? Can we leave now?'

'Not entirely,' said the Doctor. 'By which I mean... well, not at all, actually.'

'Oh,' said Amy.

'Soon, though. Definitely soon. I've been getting the measure of the computer that runs this place. I reckon I can take it!'

The Doctor unlocked the TARDIS door. Amy followed him inside.

They skirted the six-sided console, and headed for an alcove that was cluttered with chests and crates. The Doctor pulled a chest full of junk towards him. Amy watched as he scattered its contents across the floor.

'What are you looking for?' asked Amy.

'I'll know that when I find it,' said the Doctor.

He finished with the first chest and started on a second.

'Doctor, when you were in Space Traffic Control,' said Amy, 'with the cameras… you didn't happen to see where Rory might have got to?'

'I hoped you might know,' said the Doctor. 'He's your husband.'

He had found something. It was buried beneath a tangle of wires and circuit boards. The Doctor wrenched it free. 'Oh, yes,' he said. 'This should do the trick.'

Amy craned to see the device. It looked like a metal spider with a keypad on its back. She asked the Doctor what it was.

'An automated safe-cracker,' he said, jumping to his feet.

'Safe-cracker?' echoed Amy. 'For cracking safes? And you just happen to have one of those lying about the place?'

'Why not?' The Doctor grinned. 'You never know when you might have to break into a safe. Or out of one. Did I ever tell you about that time on Fortis Major?'

'So, what does it do exactly?' asked Amy.

'Runs through about five hundred combinations per second,' said the Doctor. 'Wire this into the computers in Space Traffic Control and…'

'And it'll find the security codes we need to lift the quarantine and release the docking clamps and send everyone home!'

'In forty minutes or less, or your money back.'

'Well, in that case,' said Amy, 'why are we standing here?'

'Of course,' said the Doctor, as he and Amy walked away from the TARDIS, 'we aren't entirely out of the woods yet.'

'What's that supposed to mean?' asked Amy.

The Doctor nodded to their right. A Despond had just stepped out from between two luggage carousels. Its nose and ears twitched as it saw them.

Amy shook her head. 'It can't be… they can't be hungry again already!'

'I suspect,' said the Doctor, 'that the Desponds have a very efficient metabolism. Either that or they found a packet of antacid tablets in the duty-free shop. Amy…'

'I remember. "Try to worry.'

It worked last time, thought Amy. *Just have to close my eyes and concentrate – tell myself there is no hope. There is no hope!*

'I wasn't going to say that, actually,' said the Doctor. 'I was going to say that, when I say, "run", you should run back to the TARDIS.'

Amy opened her eyes a fraction. 'You were "going to say"?'

'Before I saw the other one.'

Amy looked properly now. A second Despond had appeared from behind the TARDIS. It was cutting off their retreat.

There is no hope, Amy told herself fiercely. But, this time, it wasn't working. This time, the Doctor was here by her side. So, how could things be hopeless?

'Plan B,' said the Doctor. 'When I say "run", you just… run. I'll try to draw the Desponds away from you. *Run!*'

Amy ran for it. A Despond began to follow her, but the Doctor leapt into its path.

'Here, boy,' said the Doctor. 'Come to me. Not… quite so fast…'

Now, it was his turn to flee, with the Desponds at his heels.

The Doctor ran for the working carousel, and jumped onto it. It carried him away from his pursuers, while leaving his feet free.

The Desponds kept pace with the carousel, snarling and snapping at the Doctor's ankles. He tried to push them away with the soles of his shoes.

One of them leapt up, and caught the Doctor's trouser leg between its teeth. It yanked him backwards off his feet. The Doctor landed on the carousel on his back.

The Desponds jumped on top of him. They opened their mouths to reveal their slavering feeding tentacles.

Amy cried out, 'Doctor!' She started towards him.

He was fighting off the Desponds. He pushed one of them away from him. Its three paws skittered on the moving carousel, and it fell off it sideways.

The Despond landed on the floor between Amy and the Doctor. She backed away from it, nervously. She had no hope of reaching the Doctor now.

The other Despond had dug its front claws into its victim's chest. It sank its feeding tentacle into the Doctor's throat.

Then, both the Doctor and the Despond were carried away by the luggage carousel, through an opening in the wall and out of Amy's sight.

CHAPTER 9
ONCE BITTEN

Amy eyed the Despond that sat between her and the luggage carousel.

The Despond eyed her in return. Then, it stood up and burped loudly.

The Despond waddled away, towards the departure lounge. It looked a little bit wobbly, as if it had eaten too much.

No, thought Amy. *That can't have happened — not to him!*

She ran up to the moving carousel, as it brought the Doctor around to her again.

He was lying on his back on the carousel, sucking his thumb — and Amy couldn't miss the big red suction mark on his throat.

She buried her face in her hands, in despair.

The Desponds had fed again. They had taken the Doctor's hope!

Rory was standing inside a tiny airlock. He was elbow to elbow with Roger.

Two drums of cable were fastened to the wall. Roger clipped one cable to a loop on his spacesuit and another to Rory's.

Roger pointed out a tiny explosive charge, stuck to Rory's cable drum. 'One word from me,' he said, 'and Cap will blow that charge from the cockpit. It'll burn right through your lifeline.'

'Yeah,' said Rory. 'I got that.'

For the past two minutes, he had been able to hear machinery: the grinding and wheezing of an air pump. Now, the pump shut off with a final clunk.

It had done its job. A gauge on the wall showed that there was no atmosphere left inside the airlock. Rory and Roger's oxygen tanks were the only things keeping them alive. Rory swallowed nervously.

The spaceship's artificial gravity had also been shut off, and Rory was floating. His heavy tool kit was floating too, no longer weighing him down.

Roger spun the locking wheel of the outer airlock door. He pushed it open. He took the hesitant Rory by the arm and gave him a decisive push – out into space!

'Doctor, please,' Amy pleaded, 'get up!'

She managed to drag him off the moving carousel, but it was like handling a rag doll. He sagged to the floor, and sat there with his chin on his knees.

'No point,' said the Doctor.

'Don't be daft! You can fight this, Doctor. I know you can fight it! We have the safe-cracker now, remember? That means we can…'

'Oh, that,' said the Doctor. 'I don't think that will work.'

'What do you mean? You said…'

'It was in that chest for about a hundred years. It's probably seized up by now. And, anyway, I've been thinking, and I think we shouldn't interfere.'

'Can you even hear yourself?'

The Doctor looked up at Amy. 'Don't you see?' he said. 'This terminal was placed under quarantine for a reason: to keep the Desponds contained. If we lift it…'

'We have to lift it! We have to let all these people go!'

'We'd be letting the Desponds go too. They'd be bound to slip aboard a ship and…'

'They won't! We'll make sure they don't!'

'And then they'll spread across the galaxy,' the Doctor shuddered at the thought. 'And I almost let that happen. What could I have been thinking?'

'You were trying to help,' said Amy. 'You're the Doctor. It's what you do.'

The Doctor shook his head. 'Not any more. A quiet life for me, from now on. No risks. You know, I can't remember the last time I just sat and watched the telly with a nice plate of cheese on toast. Do you think I should buy some comfy slippers?'

'Oh, right,' said Amy. 'That does it!' She took the Doctor's arm again. She hauled him to his feet. 'So, what do you want to do?' she challenged him. 'Give up?'

'Yes, I think we should,' said the Doctor.

'Get back into the TARDIS and just… just fly out of here?'

'That would probably be for the best.'

'What about Janie, Doctor? What about Mr and Mrs Henry and the others? You'd be leaving them to starve!'

'I suppose I would.'

'You promised them you'd save them!'

'I know. I know I did. But I've tried my best and I can't do it.' The Doctor put his hands on Amy's shoulders. He looked right into her eyes, and she saw only despair in his gaze. 'So, I think you're right,' he said. 'We should leave.'

'No! No, Doctor, I didn't mean…'

But the Doctor was already heading for the TARDIS.

'Nothing more we can do here, Pond,' he said over his shoulder. 'It's hopeless!'

Cap's spaceship had probably been white once. Now, its hull was all corroded and patched up with black tape. Rory certainly wouldn't have wanted to fly in it. Not that flying outside of it was any better.

Rory flapped about helplessly in zero-gravity. He wanted to be sick. He dropped his toolbox, and it floated away from him. Fortunately, Roger caught it.

The security guard was sticking close to his prisoner.

Roger took Rory's arm. He found a handhold on the side of the ship. He used it to pull the two of them along the hull, toward the nose.

Rory found that, if he faced the ship, he felt better.

The ship was attached, via a white docking tube, to the spaceport itself. The spaceport looked like a giant white top. Its 'spindle', Rory guessed, was the Space Traffic Control tower. He wondered if the Doctor and Amy were in there now.

He wondered if they were watching him.

There were portholes in the side of the spaceport. Through these, Rory could see the lights of the departure lounge. He could see people in there, and he thought he could make out Mr and Mrs Henry. He focused on them.

It was when he looked the other way that Rory had problems. It was when he looked out at the endless darkness of space. That was when he felt alone. That was when he felt small. That was when his stomach insisted on performing somersaults.

Roger had reached an engine pod. He thrust the toolbox into Rory's chest. *'Go on then, genius,'* his voice came over the helmet radio. *'Show us what you can do.'*

Rory almost floated right past the pod. He had to grab hold of it to steady himself. He opened the toolbox. He looked at its collection of different-sized spanners and screwdrivers and gadgets he didn't even recognise.

He looked at the engine pod: an egg-shaped bulge on the side of the spaceship, roughly where the wing would have been on an aeroplane.

Rory had planned to tinker with the engines a little, maybe tighten a few nuts and bolts. At least it would have looked like he was trying. He realised, now, that even this was beyond his talents.

There must be a tool in the box that would open up the pod – but Rory had no idea which one it might be.

Roger was glaring at him, impatiently. Any second now, he would realise the truth: that Rory really couldn't help him. And then…?

If Rory was ever going to act, it had to be now.

He thrust the toolbox into Roger's face. Its contents spilled out, more gently than Rory had hoped they might. They floated around the security guard's head, doing him no harm but at least keeping him distracted for a second.

Rory pulled himself along his lifeline, as fast as he could. He had to get back on board the ship before Roger could recover and radio Cap in the cockpit.

In his haste, however, he overshot the airlock door.

Rory could hear Roger screaming in his ear. *'He's making a break for it, Cap. Cut the lifeline. Cut the lifeline!'*

He heard Cap's much calmer response: *'Will do, son. Cap out.'*

Rory managed to turn himself around. He pulled on his lifeline again, but the cable went slack in his hands. He kept tugging on it anyway, out of desperation.

He reeled in the cable, until he was holding its burnt end. He stared at it in horror.

His momentum kept him drifting backwards, past the tail of the ship. He tried to get back. He kicked his legs like a swimmer, but he had nothing to push against.

'I warned you what would happen,' Roger's radio voice sneered in Rory's ear.

Rory was moving even faster than he had

thought. He was getting further and further away from Cap's spaceship. *And from the spaceport too*, he realised.

He felt as if his heart had frozen in his chest. *They did it*, he thought. *Roger and Cap actually did it… They've sent me hurtling off into outer space!*

The Doctor paused in the TARDIS doorway. He turned back to Amy.

'Coming?' he asked.

'You can't be serious,' said Amy.

'Deadly.'

'But what about Rory? Apart from anything else…'

The Doctor shrugged. 'He's probably in some kind of trouble. Nothing we can do.'

'That's my husband you're talking about!'

'And, if we go looking for him, we'll probably get into trouble ourselves and then we'll never get out of here and… No. This is how it has to be. No choice. I'm leaving. Right now. So, are you coming with me, Amy Pond?'

'No,' said Amy. She folded her arms stubbornly. 'No, I'm not.'

The Doctor nodded. 'Okay,' he said.

He slammed the TARDIS door in Amy's face.

'And you won't go either,' Amy shouted through the door. 'I know you won't – because whatever those monsters have done to you, whatever they've taken from you, you're still *him*. You're the Doctor. You're my Doctor.'

The TARDIS engines wheezed and groaned into life. The light on its roof was flashing. Amy's heart was pounding.

'You're my Raggedy Doctor,' she cried, 'and I'm Amelia Pond, the girl who waited, and I know you'd never abandon me. You always come back for me!'

She went to hammer on the police box doors. Her fist went through them.

The engine noise was building to a raucous trumpeting.

The TARDIS was leaving without Amy.

CHAPTER 10
ADRIFT

Amy could see right through the TARDIS now. It was almost gone.

Then, something wonderful happened. The TARDIS came back.

Its blue box shape became darker and more solid before Amy's eyes. The noise of its engine faded, and the blue light on the roof went out.

The police box door opened. The Doctor was leaning against the doorway. He looked wretched. 'I don't think I want to go,' he said.

Amy grinned in relief. 'You see?' she said. 'You can't ever leave me. You're stuck with me, buster. You and me, forever.'

'Help me,' said the Doctor.

'Always,' Amy promised.

Rory fought the urge to panic.

It wasn't easy. He wanted to scream. But with every second that passed, he was drifting further and further out into space. He needed to think fast.

Maybe someone in the spaceport will look out of a porthole, he thought. *Maybe they'll see me out here and raise the alarm – before I drift out of sight!*

He had pleaded for help over his helmet radio, but had had no reply. Either Roger was ignoring him or Rory was already out of his radio range.

He wondered how much oxygen he had left in his tank. *Not much, I'll bet!*

No one was going to help him. Rory had to help himself. He had to find a way to brake; better still, to reverse the direction of his flight.

Only one way occurred to him, and it was incredibly dangerous.

Rory felt he had no choice. He turned his back to the spaceport. He was careful to use only tiny movements, so he wouldn't send himself into a spin.

He felt along the tube that connected his oxygen tank to his chest unit. He found the end of the tube and he twisted it.

He pulled the air tube out of its socket. He aimed it in front of him like a fire hose. Rory couldn't see the oxygen that rushed out of the end of the tube, but he could feel its effects. His stomach heaved as he was propelled backwards like a rocket.

He collided with the spaceport, hard.

If it hadn't been for Rory's padded spacesuit, he might have been badly hurt. As it was, his ribs ached and it took him half a minute to find his breath.

By that time, he had lost a great deal of oxygen. Rory clung to the side of the spaceport with one hand, as he tried – and failed – to reconnect his air tube with the other. When the tube stopped fighting him, he knew it was too late. His oxygen tank was empty. He had only the air in his helmet.

He had to get inside the spaceport. He looked

for a way in.

To his relief, he found one. An airlock door! Now, he just had to reach it.

Rory struck out towards the door. He found plenty of hand- and footholds on the spaceport's side. He climbed from one of them to the other, careful never to lose contact for fear of drifting off again.

He had certainly been noticed now. A mass of curious passengers had been drawn to the departure lounge portholes, to watch Rory's halting progress across them.

He was starting to feel light-headed again.

Is it my imagination or is it getting hard to breathe?

He was sure he wasn't going to make it. Then, at last, the locking wheel of the airlock door was in Rory's hands. He spun it round and yanked open the door. He pulled himself into the airlock and slammed the door shut behind him.

Rory's chest ached. He could see dark spots on the edges of his vision. But, as he sagged to his knees, he heard the most beautiful sound in the world.

He heard the sound of an air pump activating.

Rory was still weak at the knees as he stumbled into the spaceport departure lounge. He was grateful to be alive, though, and to be breathing warm, sweet air.

He had left his helmet behind in the airlock. He dropped into a red plastic seat and began to strip off the rest of the spacesuit.

'So, this is where you've been hiding yourself.'

Mr Henry had appeared in the seat beside Rory. Mrs Henry sat at his other side.

'Mr Henry and I have been worried about you, dear,' she said. 'You missed out on all the excitement.'

Mr Henry peered closely at Rory. 'Did the Desponds get you? Oh, yes. They fed on you, didn't they?'

'No, actually,' said Rory. 'The Desponds didn't feed on me.'

'Are you sure?' Mr Henry frowned. 'Because you look pretty hopeless to me.'

'I'm not… the Desponds haven't fed on me!
I've been… I was onboard one of the spaceships,
actually – with that security guard, Roger.'

Mr and Mrs Henry looked at each other. There
was fear in their eyes.

'Well, aren't you going to ask me?' asked Rory.
'Aren't you going to ask me, "What were you doing
onboard a spaceship, Rory?"'

The Henrys said nothing.

'No,' said Rory. 'You don't dare ask, do you?
You don't want to know, in case the answer gives
you hope. Well, you don't have to worry about
that. Roger and his friend, Cap, they have enough
hope for all of us – and, if someone doesn't stop
them, they're going to tear this spaceport apart
with it.'

The Doctor had gone back into the TARDIS. He
had been in such a hurry, though, that he had left
his key in the door lock. *I'll take that*, decided Amy,
snatching it on her way past. *It'll be safer with me
for the moment!*

The Doctor was already at the console. She ran up there to join him. 'Er, what do you think you're doing?' she asked.

He was flicking switches and pushing buttons. He turned to Amy with an intense stare. 'Stop me!' he breathed.

He was setting flight coordinates. He was trying to leave again.

'Doctor, no!' cried Amy. She got between him and the controls. She wrestled his left hand away from them, but he reached around her with his right.

'I can't help myself!' said the Doctor. 'Whenever I think about Terminal 4000 and the Desponds, it's like…'

He was dashing around the console, operating controls as he went. Amy couldn't keep up with him.

'It's like a yawning great chasm in my stomach. No, a void. It's like a void. An aching void. Of despair. And I can't stand it, Amy. I have to get away from it!'

Amy lunged at the Doctor. She grabbed his head in her hands. She planted a big kiss on his lips.

The Doctor reeled away from Amy, aghast. 'Wh-what did you just *do*?'

'I gave you something else to think about.'

'It's just any excuse with you, isn't it?' the Doctor spluttered.

'Oi, less of the complaining, please. I'll have you know, I'm an excellent kisser.'

'You're also married. And… and human. And…'

The Doctor sighed. He wandered over to the nearest set of steps, and sat down on it. He buried his face in his hands.

The kiss had worked. It had distracted the Doctor from the controls. Amy almost wished it hadn't. She hated to see him, of all people, like this. His boundless energy had left him. He looked defeated.

'You were right, Amy,' said the Doctor. 'There's no point in our leaving. We'd only wind up somewhere worse. Best we just stay here. In the TARDIS. Where it's safe. We should probably stay in here forever.'

It was just as Rory had feared.

Cap and Roger were both in the cockpit of Cap's ship. Rory could hear their muffled voices in there. He took a deep breath and pushed open the cockpit door.

Cap was sitting in the pilot's seat. Roger stood at his shoulder. He had changed out of his spacesuit, back into his uniform.

They both turned to gape at the newcomer in surprise. Roger went for his gun.

'You're supposed to be dead!' exclaimed Roger.

'And you're supposed to be a security guard,' said Rory. 'It's your job to protect people, not to kidnap them and throw them out into space and…'

'You should have stayed away, son,' Cap drawled.

'You were going to do it, weren't you?' said Rory. 'You were going to start the engines and blast your way out of here!'

'And we still are,' said Roger.

'Course,' said Cap, 'I'd be happier if you'd souped up the engines like you were supposed to. But Roger here had this notion for a new fuel mix that might…'

'I won't let you,' said Rory. 'I won't let you risk everyone's lives.'

'And how do you plan on stopping us?' sneered Roger. He cocked his gun.

'Got any bullets for that thing yet?' asked Rory.

Roger blanched. 'There're still two of us to one of you,' he said.

'Not this time,' said Rory. He could hear footsteps padding up behind him. 'This time, I brought some friends.'

Rory hadn't found it hard to get two Desponds to follow him in here. He had just had to hope they would.

He stepped aside now, and allowed the two creatures to waddle past him, into the cockpit. Cap leapt from his seat and Roger shrank against the bulkhead in horror.

Rory was relieved. He had taken a big gamble.

He had gambled that Cap and Roger — so hopeful about their escape plans — would be a bigger lure to the Desponds than he was. He had been right.

Rory faltered in the doorway, as the Desponds advanced on Cap and Roger.

'I'm sorry,' he said. 'I couldn't think of another way to… I had to make you lose hope in your plan, so you wouldn't… I mean it. I'm sorry.'

Rory closed the door behind him. He leaned against it, to make sure it stayed shut.

From inside the cockpit, he could hear the Desponds snarling and growling. He could hear the hopeless cries of their prey.

Then, after a minute or so, there was silence.

CHAPTER 11
SUPER SONIC

Rory could still hear Roger and Cap's screams in his mind.

What choice did I have, though? he asked himself. *Someone had to stop them!*

At least the Desponds were leaving him alone now. No doubt they had sensed his low spirits and knew he would be no feast for them.

Rory had asked the Henrys for directions to Space Traffic Control. He felt he had to find Amy and the Doctor.

He had just passed the TARDIS, by the luggage carousels, when he heard a familiar voice calling his name. He turned.

Amy was standing in the TARDIS doorway. She was beckoning to Rory. He could already feel his hopes rising as he ran to join her.

'What's going on?' asked Rory. 'What are you doing in here?'

'It's the Doctor,' said Amy. She closed the TARDIS door behind them.

'You aren't... we aren't leaving already? But what about...?'

Amy looked across the control room. Rory followed her gaze. He saw the Doctor, sitting on a step, with his head in his hands.

'Oh,' said Rory. 'You mean he's...? The Desponds?'

Amy nodded. They approached the Doctor together, cautiously.

'Come on, Doctor,' said Rory, with forced cheer. 'Can't sit around here all day. You've got work to do. Monsters to fight. Last-second saves to, er, carry out.'

The Doctor didn't respond.

Amy sat down beside him. 'What can we do?' she asked.

'Nothing,' said the Doctor. 'There's nothing you can do. There's no hope.'

'Of course there is,' said Amy. 'There's always hope.'

'Not this time.'

'Janie... the last time I saw Janie, she was almost optimistic again. This feeling, this hopelessness – it wears off, Doctor.'

'It doesn't feel like it will. Maybe it'll be different with me.'

'Yeah,' said Amy, 'maybe it will – cos if anyone can beat this, it's you. You've got... normally, you're just bursting with hope. It's like... it's like an inexhaustible commodity with you, Doctor. And I know... I know the Desponds could never have taken it all. There must be some hope left in you, somewhere.'

'I'm tired,' said the Doctor. 'Tired of fighting the monsters. What's the point? They always come back. There are always more monsters.'

'He does have a point there,' said Rory.

Amy shot him a look. 'Not helping,' she said.

Amy and Rory waited. It was all they could think to do.

They just waited. And hoped. They hoped the Doctor would recover in time.

The minutes crawled by. Rory paced around the console, anxiously. Amy sat beside the Doctor, holding him tight – until at last he stirred.

The Doctor took out the sonic screwdriver. He began to adjust it.

'Yes, that's it, Doctor,' said Amy. 'That's the spirit!'

The Doctor threw the sonic screwdriver down. He buried his face again. 'It's no good!'

'What? What's no good?' Amy picked up the sonic screwdriver. She pressed it back into the Doctor's hand. 'What were you trying to do? Tell me, Doctor.'

'A stupid long shot,' he muttered. 'It would never have worked.'

'What do you mean? Of course it would've…

Your plans always work. Well, almost always. And especially when there's sonicking involved. Sonicking *is* cool. That's right, isn't it, Doctor? It's almost as cool as… as bow ties and fezzes.'

The Doctor looked down at the sonic screwdriver.

'Sonicking is cool,' he conceded. 'Oh, but I tried this before – finding a sound frequency that'll repel the Desponds.'

'Sounds like a good idea to me,' said Amy. 'Sounds like a fantastic idea!'

'Thing is,' said the Doctor, 'I can't do it here. I'd have to try out different sound frequencies on the Desponds themselves. And if I tried the wrong one…'

'What'd happen?' asked Rory.

'I could bring the Desponds to me. It's what happened before.'

Amy snatched the sonic screwdriver from the Doctor. 'I'll do it!'

'Whoa,' said Rory, 'wait a second! Do you even know how to…?'

'I was watching what the Doctor did. Twist this bit here to change the frequency; push this button here to make the sound. It's not so hard.'

'Yeah, okay,' said Rory, 'but the Desponds –'

'Someone has to do something,' said Amy. 'That's the problem with this place. No one's doing anything. No one dares hope in case the Desponds feed on them – but, if no one has any hope, then how can anyone ever escape from here?'

'I'll come with you,' offered Rory.

'No,' said Amy. 'Stay here with the Doctor. Try to cheer him up. And keep him away from the controls until he's feeling more himself. I've had an idea!'

Amy stepped out of the TARDIS. There were no Desponds in sight.

She pressed the button on the sonic screwdriver. It emitted a high-pitched shriek, which set her teeth on edge.

Amy stayed close to the TARDIS. She was ready to run back inside if she had to. However, no Desponds appeared.

'Okay,' she said to herself. 'Not *attracting* the monsters. That's something.'

Amy started walking. She turned the corner into the empty main concourse, where the check-in desks were. She saw a Despond at the far end of the concourse, beneath a sign for the spaceport food court. It had overturned a bin and was playing with its contents. Amy could smell the rotting waste from here.

She approached the dog-like creature on tiptoe. She was halfway along the concourse when it saw her. It looked up from the bin, its nose twitching.

Amy aimed the sonic screwdriver at the Despond. She activated it again.

The sonic shrieked, as it had before. But the Despond appeared unaffected.

'Okay,' said Amy. 'Don't panic. Plenty of time yet.'

She twisted the sonic screwdriver and pressed the button. This time, the Despond yawned. Amy could see its feeding tentacle, with the little mouth on the end of it.

The Despond began to approach her, unhurriedly. Amy backed away from it. She tried another sound frequency, and another. The Despond kept on coming.

Amy could no longer hear the sonic screwdriver. The sounds it was making were too high for her ears to detect. Suddenly, however, the Despond froze. It whimpered.

Then, it roared.

The Despond came charging at Amy. It was foaming at the mouth. Amy was so startled that she dropped the sonic screwdriver. It skittered across the tiled floor.

Amy stooped to retrieve the device. She held it up to the oncoming Despond, but there was no time to try another sound frequency. She ran for it instead.

The Space Traffic Control tower, she thought. *Got to make it inside!*

She leapt through the door, and turned to shut it in the Despond's face. Oh no – too late! It's too close behind me!

The Despond barrelled through the door, knocking Amy over. She landed on the spiral staircase that led up to the top of the tower. The Despond lunged at her throat.

Amy kicked it in the stomach.

The Despond fell back. Amy pushed herself to her feet and scrambled up the stairs. She rounded the first bend. She froze in horror.

There was another Despond on the staircase above her. Amy was surrounded.

The Desponds closed in on her. She shrank against the wall. She fumbled with the sonic screwdriver. She gave it a good twist. She raised it above her head. She closed her eyes. She pressed the button.

The Desponds yelped and mewled. They sounded as if they were in pain. They turned and scampered away from Amy.

Amy let out the breath she had been holding. She kissed the sonic screwdriver. 'Sonicking *is* cool!' she said to herself.

Amy continued up the staircase.

She went carefully, because one of the Desponds had gone this way. She kept that button on the sonic firmly pressed.

She reached the top of the stairs. The security door was half-closed over the Space Traffic Control room. It was jammed by a chair.

Amy crouched down. She peered under the door.

She came eye to eye with the missing Despond. It had retreated into the circular control room, as Amy had expected. It had had nowhere else to go.

Amy raised the sonic screwdriver. The Despond howled, and backed away from her as far as it could.

She crawled into the control room. She stood up. The Despond had taken cover underneath an instrument console. Amy kept her back to the wall. She walked around the room slowly. The Despond trembled as she approached it.

She was careful not to get between the Despond and the exit. She didn't want to think about what the creature might do if it was cornered.

The Despond bolted, at last. It ran under the security door and disappeared down the stairs. Amy waited until she was sure it was gone. Then she laid down the sonic screwdriver and looked for the tannoy controls.

The passengers were even more subdued than normal. Many of them had returned to their seats, while others were shuffling around aimlessly.

It was always like this after a raid, thought Janie. With the fighting over, they were left to contemplate what they had gained – which, for most of them, was nothing. They were all still trapped here.

Janie was treating a young man with a cut under his eye. She had just used up the last of her antiseptic spray. Her flight attendant's first-aid kit was almost empty.

Three melodic chimes rang out, above her head. The public address system. Janie didn't even bother to look up, this time. She wouldn't be tricked into hoping again.

'Erm… so, okay, yeah. Your attention please.'

Janie was surprised to hear Amy's voice.

'This isn't a passenger announcement,' said Amy. 'I just wanted to say something, and this seemed like the best way to reach all of you.

'I want to tell you all a story. It's a sort of a fairy tale, really. It's about a... a Raggedy Doctor who travels to different worlds in a magic blue box.

'And I think you're gonna want to hear it.'

CHAPTER 12
SOMEONE TO BELIEVE IN

'Erm... so, okay, yeah. Your attention please.' Rory had turned on the TARDIS's scanner. He had wanted to see – and hear – what was happening outside, in case Amy was in trouble.

He shook the Doctor. 'Doctor. Hey. Do you hear that? That's Amy. On the tannoy. She must have reached Space Traffic Control. She's all right.'

The Doctor didn't respond.

Rory listened to Amy's voice. 'She's saying something about... a fairy tale, I think. About... oh, right. Yeah. Of course. About her Raggedy

Doctor. What else?'

'Heard it,' said the Doctor.

'Once upon a time…' said Amy. 'I was seven years old, when the Doctor crashed in my back garden. I looked out of my window, and I saw…'

She could see the departure lounge on the security monitors. A handful of the passengers had stopped to listen to her. Most were ignoring her.

They could still hear her voice, though. Short of covering their ears, they couldn't escape her voice.

Amy continued to tell her story. She related her first impressions of the Doctor, as he had climbed out of the crashed TARDIS: how he had seemed so wise and so kind and so funny and how it had been impossible not to trust him.

She talked about fish custard and a mysterious crack in her bedroom wall.

Amy had told the story so many times by now, she knew it by heart.

Rory knew the story too. He could almost mouth the words along with Amy.

He wrinkled his nose at the 'fish custard' part. 'Did you really do that?' he asked the Doctor. 'Did you really eat…? No, never mind.'

The Doctor looked at Rory, dolefully. 'What is she doing?'

'Oh, the usual,' said Rory. 'The same thing she did most days throughout our childhood. And when we dated. And on our wedding day. She's talking about you.'

'But why?'

'You tell me,' said Rory. 'She's laying it on a bit thick, don't you think? I mean, considering we just got…' He caught the Doctor's eye and shut up.

Rory sat beside the Doctor. 'Amy did say something, actually. About how people had to hope. And, if you remember, Doctor, in the departure lounge, *you* said…'

'I said that people who get to know me…'

'You said that they'd – we'd – always have hope.'

'I did say that. I remember saying that. I was so wrong.'

'No. No, you weren't wrong, Doctor. I might not always... I mean, you might not always be able to tell, but... you give me hope. No matter how bad things might have got sometimes, you've always...'

'She's... telling them about me,' the Doctor realised.

'Yes,' said Rory. 'Yes, she is. Amy's telling everyone about you. She's letting them get to know you, Doctor, so that they can start hoping again.'

'Let me tell you about hope,' said Amy. 'Because I know a thing or two about hope.

'For twelve long years – over half my life – I hoped to see the Doctor, my Raggedy Doctor, again. Even when I had everyone telling me...

'They said he wasn't real. They said I must have made him up. They said I should forget about him. But I couldn't do that. I couldn't give up on the Doctor.

'He had said he would come back for me. He had promised. And I trusted him. So, I waited. And I hoped. And then, one day… one amazing, brilliant day…

'One day, the Doctor was there. He had kept his word. And everything I'd ever hoped for – everything I'd dreamed and much, much more – it all came true for me.

'And do you know what? All the waiting, all the hoping – it was worth it! It was so, so worth it!'

'You don't believe this nonsense, do you, Mrs Henry?'

Mrs Henry started at the sound of her husband's voice. 'Oh. No, dear,' she said. 'No, of course I don't. Nonsense? What nonsense? I wasn't even listening to it.'

But she *had* been listening – and, all across the departure lounge, other people were listening too. They were listening, and talking about what they had heard. About the Doctor. And some of them were remembering the tall, floppy-haired man in tweed, who had appeared in their midst earlier. The man who had fought the Desponds. And some of them were saying they had seen a blue box, just as Amy had described it.

And some of them – a handful to begin with, but others soon followed – were wandering out into the baggage claim hall, to see this blue box for themselves.

'It won't work,' said the Doctor.

Rory looked at the scanner screen. He saw the first few passengers arriving outside the TARDIS, staring at it in awe. 'I think it already is,' he said.

'They'll only make themselves targets,' said the Doctor, 'for the Desponds.'

'But there are only twelve Desponds, remember?' said Rory. 'And how many people out there? About a hundred and sixty? And I bet... some of them, they can't have been fed on in days. They *can* still hope.'

'If they dare,' said the Doctor.

'If someone gives them a reason to try.'

'I can't be that person. I'm just a… I'm just an idiot with a blue box and a bow tie. And nice hair. I do have nice hair.'

'You don't have to give them hope,' said Rory. 'Amy's doing it already. She has enough hope for all of us.'

It was working. Amy could see it on the security monitors.

A crowd was forming around the TARDIS. Its members were still confused, uncertain. They didn't know what had brought them here – or, if they did, they were denying it to themselves. Some people, having made the trek to the TARDIS doors, had already lost their nerve and turned back.

Most of them – both there and in the departure lounge – were waiting. They were waiting to hear more. So, Amy had to keep talking. She had to tell them more stories.

Fortunately, she had plenty to tell.

She hadn't rehearsed these new stories as she had the first one. She had been too busy living them. All the same, the words came tumbling out of Amy's mouth. She told her audience about *Starship UK*, and about Winston Churchill and the Daleks.

She told them about the Weeping Angels. 'So, here I am, right,' she said, 'with these statues – these deadly living statues – all around me, and I'm blind. I mean, I'm literally blind. I can't open my eyes or I'll die. Sounds hopeless, right? Wrong. Because I felt the Doctor's hands on mine. I heard his voice, asking me to trust him.'

Amy talked about vampires in Venice. She talked about the Silurians, the Krafayis and the Cybermen. She talked about all the times she had faced great danger, and all the times the Doctor had come through for her.

And, the more Amy spoke, the more people seemed to listen.

The crowd around the TARDIS was growing by the second. Its mood had changed, too, becoming more confident, expectant. There was only one problem.

The Desponds were beginning to take notice.

Janie had been waiting for this. She had been dreading it.

Two Desponds were prowling along the edge of the departure lounge. They were approaching the steady stream of people headed for the baggage claim hall.

Janie drew her knees up to her chest, resting her heels on her seat. She closed her eyes. She didn't want to see what happened next. She waited for the screams.

She opened her eyes again.

No one had been attacked. In fact, the Desponds had backed off. One of them was scampering away. It hid under a chair.

They were afraid, Janie realised. Something had made the Desponds afraid!

Could it be possible, she wondered? Could Amy have been telling the truth, after all? Could there actually be…?

No, she told herself. *Don't finish that thought!*

All the same, Janie found herself rising to her feet. She found herself joining the stream of passengers. She was just being curious, she told herself. She only wanted to see what was happening out there.

She wasn't expecting anything.

Rory had noticed the Desponds' odd behaviour too.

He could see one of the creatures at the far end of the hall. It was keeping its distance from the crowd around the TARDIS. He pointed this out to the Doctor.

The Doctor – to Rory's surprise – stood up and joined him at the scanner screen.

'Yeah,' he muttered. 'Makes sense, I suppose.'

'What makes sense?' asked Rory. 'Why aren't the Desponds attacking?'

'A surfeit of hope,' said the Doctor.

'What?'

'The Desponds can overeat. We saw it after the riot. They can gorge themselves on hope till they're sick. And, right now, they're sensing more hope in this spaceport than they have in some time. It must be making them nervous.'

'So, they're keeping their distance.'

'For now,' said the Doctor. 'They're afraid that, once they start feeding, they won't be able to stop. It won't last, of course. Overeating is better than starving.'

'But for now,' said Rory, 'it's safe out there. Everyone is safe.'

'As long as they stay hopeful,' said the Doctor.

'So, there *is* some use in hoping, after all.'

The Doctor looked at Rory. He was about to say something, when a shout went up from outside the TARDIS: 'Doctor! Doctor! Help us, Doctor!'

The voice was a lone one, at first, but it was joined by many more. The crowd's pleas grew in volume, and merged into a rhythmic chant.

'Doctor! Doctor! Doctor!'

The Doctor stuck his fingers in his ears. 'I'm not the one they want.'

'But it's your name they're calling,' said Rory.

'I can't… what if I let them down again?'

'You won't,' said Rory. 'The only way you'll do

that is if you keep hiding from them. That's your public out there, Doctor. They're waiting for you to show yourself – and I know you wouldn't want to disappoint them.'

CHAPTER 13
FIGHT OR FLIGHT

The Doctor emerged from the TARDIS to whoops and cheers.

He was overwhelmed. He stared at the sea of faces before him. Such hopeful faces. He thought they must have the wrong man. He opened his mouth to tell them so.

But then, the Doctor remembered something.

He could feel the enthusiasm of the crowd, like a physical force. It washed over him. It re-energised him. They were chanting his name. And the Doctor *remembered*.

He remembered who he was.

Amy was watching on the security camera monitors.

She watched as a grin tugged at the Doctor's lips. She watched as he straightened his shoulders and stood tall again. *Result!* she thought.

Her throat was dry from all the talking she had done. She needed a glass of water. Amy turned to leave the Space Traffic Control room. She caught her breath.

A Despond had slipped into the room behind her. It had been sneaking up on her.

The creature froze as Amy saw it. It shifted its weight onto its back claws, about to pounce. It let out a low, menacing growl.

Amy lunged for the sonic screwdriver. She snatched it up from the office chair on which she had left it. She pointed the sonic screwdriver at the Despond. She activated it.

The Despond kept coming.

Amy took the sonic screwdriver in two hands. She pressed on the button with both thumbs, as hard as she could. Still, nothing happened.

No shrieking sound. No bright green light. The sonic screwdriver was dead.

A Despond dared approach the passengers outside the TARDIS. A few people, on the edge of the crowd, were starting to look worried.

'Oh, don't mind him,' said the Doctor. 'That's as close as he can get. TARDIS force field, you see. I extended it around us. It's invisible. An invisible force field. But it'll keep the Desponds away while we chat.'

The crowd relaxed. The Doctor raised himself on tiptoes to count them.

'So, how many of you are here? About half, I'd say. Half the people in the spaceport. Okay. Could be better, could be worse. Let me answer the question you're all asking yourselves. Yes, I can get you out of here. There's only one condition.'

The lone Despond slinked away as the crowd pressed forward, eager to hear more.

'Everyone gets saved,' said the Doctor. 'That's it. That's my condition. No one gets left behind.

Not even if they want to be. Not even if they're hiding, curled up in a corner, begging to be left alone because they've no hope left.

'We're all in this together. That means we have to work together and watch out for each other. No more petty rivalries. Those of you hoarding food: share it with the hungry. Those with first aid skills and equipment: do what you can for the wounded. Those of you who can fly a spaceship: we'll be needing you shortly. Now, then.'

The Doctor surveyed the crowd again. He spied a familiar face. 'Janie Collins!' he exclaimed. 'I'm glad you could make it. Everyone knows Janie, right? Good. Because she'll be in charge of the evacuation.'

Janie shifted uncomfortably on the spot.

'I want the rest of the flight attendants to report to Janie,' said the Doctor. 'I want every passenger in Terminal 4000 accounted for, and assigned to one of the three spaceships docked out there. I want each of those ships to have a crew.'

'What about the rest of us?' someone asked.

'The rest of you… Okay, there is some bad news. Just a bit. A teensy tiny little bit.' The Doctor took a deep breath. 'I was lying about the TARDIS force field.'

A gasp of horror went up at that statement.

'But it's all right,' said the Doctor, 'because you lot, you can protect yourselves. You all saw that Despond just now. You saw how it retreated with its tail between its legs. Well, you did that, all of you – by sticking together. You did it by hoping together.'

'He's right,' someone spoke up. 'The Doctor's right.'

'Remember when the Desponds appeared? Remember that security guard? What was his name? Roger. He shot one of them.'

'The Desponds are just dumb animals. If we all stood up to them…'

'There are more of us than there are of them.'

'Problem is, we've been too busy squabbling with each other and…'

'They can't drain all of us at once!'

Rory had stepped out of the TARDIS beside the Doctor. He murmured in the Doctor's ear: 'Doctor, have you noticed? Amy…'

'Yeah,' said the Doctor. 'I noticed. She stopped talking.'

'She should have made it back by now,' said Rory. 'I'll go up there and see…'

The Doctor held Rory back. 'No,' he said. 'I need you here.' He nodded towards the crowd. 'They need you here. Things could still get nasty.'

'How do you mean?' asked Rory.

But the Doctor was already in motion. He was threading his way through the crowd.

People tugged at his sleeve. They asked him where he was going. They pleaded with him to stay. The Doctor pulled clear of them. He produced the spider-shaped safe-cracker from his pocket. He brandished it for all to see.

'I'm going up to Space Traffic Control,' announced the Doctor. 'I'm going to end the quarantine of this spaceport. In forty minutes or less, or your money back.'

The crowd was stunned into silence. He could hardly blame them.

'Oh, yeah,' said the Doctor. 'One more thing. When I said we'd be needing pilots… that would be now, in fact. At least three of them. To prepare for departure.'

The Doctor turned on his heel. He marched away, towards the control tower.

He was encouraged along his path by a thunderous wave of applause.

Amy gave the sonic screwdriver a shake. It rattled.

She remembered dropping it, downstairs in the main concourse. What if she had broken it? What if she had loosened something inside it?

Without the sonic screwdriver, she was helpless.

The Despond leapt at Amy.

She moved at the same time. She pushed an office chair into the creature's path. The Despond collided with the back of the chair and was winded.

Amy ran for the exit, but the Despond beat her to it. She fell back, across the round room. The Despond kept its beady eyes fixed on her all the way.

The creature came at her again. It leapt up onto the chair this time, using the seat as a springboard to Amy's throat.

Taken by surprise, Amy threw up her hands and shrieked as the Despond flew at her. Its feeding tentacle lashed her cheek. It left a patch of cold, green slime.

The Despond clawed at Amy's face. She pushed it away from her. The Despond fell towards an instrument panel.

There was a bang and a bright white flash.

The Despond slid off the console. It hit the floor, dead. It took Amy a moment to take in what had happened. The creature had been electrocuted!

Her eyes were drawn to a line of text, which scrolled across a tiny read-out screen:

"Alien infestation detected and neutralised."

Amy looked down at the Despond. She felt a lump forming in her throat. In death, it didn't look like a dangerous monster. It looked like a harmless pet.

The passengers returned to the departure lounge. Now, however, it was with a new sense of purpose – and the lounge was soon buzzing with activity.

Janie had gathered all the flight attendants together, as the Doctor had said. They were drawing up lists.

A crew had already been assembled. They were buttoning up their uniforms, straightening their ties. They headed for one of the idle spaceships. They found a Despond in their path. It lay in front of the airlock door, licking its paws.

Five young men came forward. They had armed themselves with sticks and chairs. They surrounded the Despond. They poked at it and jeered.

The Despond didn't like it. It climbed to its feet and snarled at its tormentors. When that didn't work, the creature backed away from them.

The men formed a human wall between the Despond and the flight crew. The grateful crew boarded their ship and shut the airlock door behind them.

A score of passengers swarmed to the portholes. They waited for over a minute.

Then a rousing cheer was raised as the spaceship's running lights came on.

Mr and Mrs Henry found Rory by the washrooms.

'You look to be at a loose end, dear,' said Mrs Henry.

'I'm… supervising,' said Rory defensively. 'What about the pair of you, anyway? I didn't see either of you at the meeting.'

'Oh, we don't get involved in business like that,' said Mr Henry.

'We don't like to get our hopes up,' Mrs Henry agreed.

'Not that we don't wish you all the very best of luck.'

'It has been a long time – hasn't it, Mr Henry?'

'Indeed. It must be two months at least since the last escape attempt.'

'There is one thing though, dear,' said Mrs Henry. 'We did say we would ask.'

Rory looked at the couple suspiciously. 'What is it?'

'We were talking to some well-mannered young chaps over there,' said Mr Henry.

Rory followed the direction of his nod. He saw the five young men who had warded off the Despond. They were looking over at him, expectantly.

He had a very bad feeling about this.

'It's just, they know you arrived here with the Doctor,' said Mrs Henry.

'And they saw you talking to us earlier,' said Mr Henry, 'and they wondered...'

Mrs Henry leaned forward and whispered, 'They've come up with a plan, you see, and they were hoping – I mean, *thinking*! They were thinking you might help them.'

From behind his back, Mr Henry produced a walking stick.

He handed the stick to Rory.

'They were thinking you might join them,' said Mr Henry, 'on a Despond hunt.'

CHAPTER 14
HIJACK

'Blimey!' exclaimed the Doctor. 'What happened here, then?'

He looked at the dead Despond on the floor of the round control room. 'Never mind,' he said. 'I get the gist.'

'Did you bring the safe-cracker?' Amy was still shaken, but trying not to show it.

The Doctor showed her the spider-shaped device. 'No more wasting time,' he said.

'What can I do?' Amy asked.

The Doctor ducked beneath a console. 'Find Rory,' he said. 'He could use your help. You know what happened the last time he was left on his own.'

'Right,' said Amy. 'It's good to have you back, Doctor.'

'Uh-huh.' The Doctor wasn't listening. He was busy wiring the safe-cracker into the console's innards.

Amy got down on her hands and knees, to crawl under the security door.

'You should keep the sonic screwdriver with you,' said the Doctor, 'for protection.'

'Ah,' said Amy. 'Yeah. I meant to say, actually. About the sonic…'

Rory had found a Despond.

It was huddled under one of the red plastic seats in the departure lounge.

He prodded it with Mr Henry's walking stick. It abandoned its makeshift shelter. It looked at Rory, warily.

It's more nervous than I am, he thought.

For the hundredth time, Rory wondered how he had been roped into this.

The plan was simple enough. It made sense,

too. The objective was to trap as many Desponds as possible behind closed doors – out of the way – before the spaceships began to board.

This meant, to begin with, that somebody had to lure a Despond into the duty-free shop. And everyone had agreed that Rory – as the Doctor's friend – was the man for the job. Well, of course they had!

The Despond was growing in confidence. It was beginning to realise that Rory was alone. It could feed on him safely, without risk of overeating.

Rory backed away slowly, and the Despond followed.

He had done this before, he reminded himself. He had led two Desponds onto Cap's ship. He knew exactly what to do. He only had to keep his cool.

The Despond quickened its pace. Rory discouraged it with another prod of the walking stick. He had reached the duty-free shop now.

He backed up through the doorway, trampling debris underfoot. He saw Mr and Mrs Henry standing behind the tills.

'What are you two doing in here?' whispered Rory.

'We're just watching dear,' said Mrs Henry.

'Mrs Henry and I are rather curious to see if this scheme of yours works.'

'We don't care either way, mind.'

'No, indeed not,' Mr Henry agreed. 'We aren't hoping for anything.'

The Despond faltered in the doorway. Perhaps it had sensed, somehow, what was waiting for it inside the shop. Rory had to lure it in.

'Here, boy,' he said, pointing to his own throat. 'Nice, um, fillet of Rory for you, packed with juicy hope… although not too much hope, because we all know that's bad for you. Just a small amount of hope that what I'm doing here might not be as completely insane as it seems, although it probably…'

The Despond came at Rory with an ear-splitting howl.

It was much faster than he had expected! Rory

leapt back and stumbled over an upturned shelving unit. He fell onto his back.

Rory couldn't see the Despond, but he could certainly hear it. He swung Mr Henry's walking stick in a blind arc, but missed his target. The Despond ducked under the stick and jumped on top of Rory. It dug its claws into his chest.

The Despond's feeding tentacle shot out. It attached itself to Rory's throat.

Amy was on her way back to the departure lounge.

She passed the TARDIS and came to the security gate. She found a man there, leaning against the wall. The man had tightly-curled hair and a thin moustache. Amy knew the face, but she couldn't recall his name.

'You're the Doctor's friend, aren't you?' said the man.

'I'm Amy.'

'Got a message for you, from your husband. He said he was waiting for you inside the box.' The man nodded towards the TARDIS.

'Oh,' said Amy. 'Right. Thanks, um…'

The man peeled back the jacket he was wearing, to reveal his security guard's uniform. 'Roger,' he said. 'Roger McDowell. Spaceport Security.'

Rory's fellow Despond hunters sprang their ambush.

The five young men leapt out from behind the still-standing shelves. They waved their makeshift weapons at the Despond.

It retracted its feeding tentacle and tried to run, but it found itself surrounded.

Someone had smashed a perfume bottle, and the scent was confusing the Despond.

Rory climbed to his feet. He felt giddy after his close escape. He raised Mr Henry's walking stick in case he had to defend himself.

The Despond was pivoting on its single front leg, snapping at anyone who dared get too close to it. But two of Rory's allies had a blanket. They cast it over the Despond.

The hunters fell upon the blinded creature and

raised their sticks to hit it.

'Enough,' cried Rory. 'That's enough!'

The hunters withdrew, reluctantly. The Despond had stopped moving. It was still conscious, though. They could all see it trembling through the blanket.

Mr Henry stepped forward. 'What on earth have you stopped for?' he demanded. 'You have it at your mercy! Kill it! Kill it before it can...'

'No,' said Rory. 'There's no need.'

'No need? After all the suffering these monsters have caused us?'

'Mr Henry is quite right, dear,' said Mrs Henry.

'Give me that blessed stick. I'll do the job myself if nobody else will!'

Mr Henry tried to snatch his walking stick back. Rory held on to it.

'The plan was to trap the Despond,' he said, 'not kill it. Well, we've done that. All we have to do now is leave the shop and close the doors – both doors – behind us.'

Mr Henry wasn't happy. He grumbled something to himself. However, he did back down.

His wife put her arm around him, and they headed for the door.

The Henrys stopped in their tracks.

There were two more Desponds in front of them.

'Back door,' Rory shouted. 'Quick!'

One of the hunters was ahead of him. He ran to the back of the shop, where there was a fire exit. He yanked it open. He found a fourth Despond behind it.

He recoiled. He tried to close the door, but the Despond was already through it. The hunter fell back to rejoin Rory and the others.

'Where are they all coming from?' cried Mrs Henry.

'It's like the Doctor said,' Rory realised. 'The Desponds are empathically linked. When we hurt that one, it must have brought the others running.'

'I knew it,' Mr Henry stormed. 'I knew we should have killed the filthy beast!'

'There's no way out!' cried one of the hunters. 'We're caught in our own trap!'

The Desponds were closing in around them.

Amy knocked on the TARDIS door. There was no answer. She hoped that nothing was wrong in there. She remembered that she still had the Doctor's key. She opened the door with it, but could see no sign of Rory in the console room.

She heard footsteps running up behind her.

Roger grabbed hold of Amy. He clamped a hand over Amy's mouth, so she couldn't cry out. He pushed her into the TARDIS.

Amy broke free of Roger. She rounded on him. 'What do you think you're doing?'

Roger pulled a gun on Amy. 'I'm getting out of here,' he said.

'We all are,' said Amy. 'We're all getting out of here'

'No. I'm getting out of here *now*. In this… what did you call it? This magic box of yours. And you're going to pilot it for me, or…'

'Hang on,' said Amy. 'Didn't someone say you'd run out of bullets?'

Roger lowered his gun, frustrated. 'Does everyone know about that?'

'All right. Fun's over,' said Amy. 'Let's go back outside, wait for the Doctor to lift the quarantine, and we'll say no more about…'

She tried to leave. Roger got in her way.

'I know what you're planning,' he said. 'You want to get rid of me. You want to feed me to the Desponds, like your husband tried to.'

This was news to Amy.

'I had a plan,' said Roger. 'I had a spaceship and a pilot. Now, he's useless. I'm only lucky the Desponds filled up on his hope and didn't feed on me too.'

'We've got spaceships,' said Amy, 'and pilots.'

'And a dozen Desponds running about the place,' said Roger. 'Don't you think we've tried to escape before?'

'It'll be different this time,' said Amy.

'I'm not taking that chance. If this box… if it does half of what you said it does…'

Amy shook her head firmly. 'Not a chance, pal,' she said.

'We could just slip away, the two of us.'

'I couldn't fly the TARDIS even if I wanted to. If you'd listened more closely to my story, you'd know that. The Doctor's the only one who can…'

'I don't believe you!'

'Well, newsflash for you, Roger: I don't care if you believe me or not!'

Amy went for the door again. She pushed Roger aside.

'I… I'll do it myself then,' said Roger. 'I'll fly this thing myself. It can't be that hard to work out the controls.'

He ran up the steps to the console. Amy cried after him, 'Roger, no! You don't know what you're doing. You could…'

Roger flicked a few switches. He pulled a lever. 'Then help me,' he said. 'Show me what to do. Because, until you do, I'm just going to keep…'

The TARDIS made a stuttering, coughing sound, and the floor beneath Amy's feet shifted. The glass-like rotor in the centre of the console shuddered violently.

Amy raced up to the TARDIS console. She yanked Roger away from it, hard enough to send him sprawling. 'What did you do?' she yelled at him. '*What did you do?*'

CHAPTER 15
CORNERED

The Doctor had wired the safe-cracker into the computer systems. He was waiting impatiently for it to do its work.

He needed something to keep his hands busy. He picked up the broken sonic screwdriver, which Amy had left behind. He swiftly took the device apart.

The Doctor soon found the problem: just a loose wire.

Normally, of course, he would have used the sonic screwdriver to fix it!

He searched his pockets. He found an old stick of chewing gum from the 1970s.

'It'll do the job,' he decided. He sat down, cross-legged, on the floor.

Had the Doctor been less absorbed in his task, he might have glanced at the security camera monitors behind him. He might have seen the TARDIS, in the baggage claim hall. He might have seen the blue light on its roof beginning to flash.

'Mr Henry,' Mrs Henry wailed, 'hold me!'

The Henrys, the five young hunters and Rory stood back to back in the ruins of the duty-free shop. Four Desponds circled the group, sizing them up. Any second now, they would choose their first victim.

Mr Henry acted first.

He gave the hunter next to him a firm push. Taken by surprise, the young man stumbled forward. He tripped over a Despond and landed on his hands and knees.

The Desponds pounced on him.

'What are you doing?' cried Rory.

'Saving our skins,' Mr Henry retorted. 'Now, while they're distracted!' He grabbed his wife's hand and ran for the fire exit.

The hunters tried to drive the Desponds away from their friend. They weren't having much luck. A feeding tentacle had found the unlucky victim's throat.

A Despond broke away from the pack. It cut in front of the fleeing Henrys, bringing them to a startled halt.

Mr Henry looked at Rory. Rory saw an evil glint in the old man's eyes.

'Oh no you don't,' he said, as Mr Henry tried to push him.

'If you had any decency,' said Mr Henry, 'you'd sacrifice yourself for the rest of us. It's your fault we're in this predicament, after all.'

'How is it my fault?'

Rory had just got Mr Henry off him when another Despond came snapping at his ankles. He swiped at it with Mr Henry's walking stick, and the Despond withdrew.

'Anyway,' said Rory, 'I've had a better idea.'

Along the side of the shop, a row of full-length windows looked out onto the departure lounge. Rory turned and flung the walking stick at the nearest of them.

The stick smashed through the shop window.

The TARDIS's engines were screeching and grinding.

Amy stared at the bewildering array of controls on the console. She wished she had paid more attention when the Doctor was using them.

'There has to be a brake on this thing,' she muttered.

Her eyes were drawn to a large lever, in the down position. Roger's hand had been near that lever. Had he pulled it?

Amy had to do something. She pushed the lever back up. The TARDIS gave one final judder and fell still.

Roger had picked himself up. He approached the console again. Amy pushed him away. 'Listen to me, you idiot. This is a complex alien machine. You can't just… you could have got us both killed! Or stranded anywhere in space or time.'

'I don't care,' said Roger. 'Anywhere is better than Terminal 4000.'

'Yeah? You fancy materialising in the heart of a sun, or… or being stranded in prehistoric times? Or…?'

Roger lunged for the controls. Amy got in his way.

'Seriously,' she warned him. 'I will hurt you.'

'Is that…?' Roger was looking past Amy. 'Is that where we are?'

She thought it might be a trick at first. She glared at Roger, suspiciously.

Then, she turned. She saw that the scanner screen had been left on. And it was no longer showing an image of the baggage check hall.

The Henrys made for the broken window. A Despond bounded after them.

The route to the fire exit door was left clear.

Two hunters gave up the struggle with the other three Desponds and ran for it.

The monsters had finished with their first victim – but they weren't satisfied yet! They were taking their chance to eat again, while they could.

One of them tackled Mrs Henry. It caught the trailing end of her floral-patterned dress between its teeth. Mrs Henry shrieked as the Despond pulled her over. She landed facedown, and flailed helplessly.

Mr Henry turned back for his wife. When he saw the Despond clawing at her, however, fear froze him.

'I'm sorry, my dear,' he said. He turned and dived out through the broken window.

Rory had been turning this way and that, not sure what to do. Now, he saw an intact perfume bottle. He snatched it up and threw it. The bottle smashed on the floor beside Mrs Henry. Her Despond attacker had a sneezing fit, and let go of her.

Rory ran up to Mrs Henry. He hauled her to

her feet. She was completely unresponsive. She had closed her eyes, and she was whimpering and moaning. She was also as heavy as she looked.

Rory had to half-carry, half-drag Mrs Henry through the debris. He bundled her out through the window, and stumbled through it after her.

Mr Henry was waiting for them in the departure lounge. He had recovered his walking stick and picked up a red plastic chair. Mrs Henry fell into his arms, howling.

Mr Henry brushed her aside. He set his chair down in front of the shop. He climbed up onto it. Rory saw what he was doing.

'Wait,' he cried. 'There are people still in there.'

With the end of his walking stick, Mr Henry had hooked a steel security shutter. He was pulling the shutter down over the broken window.

'The Desponds have them,' he insisted. 'We can't help them now.'

'You heard the Doctor,' said Rory. 'No one gets left behind.'

'They shouldn't have provoked the Desponds.

They brought this fate upon themselves!'

Mr Henry stepped down from his chair. He started to push the security shutter the rest of the way down. Before he could close it fully, Rory ducked underneath it.

Back into the duty-free shop.

Inside the shop, one Despond was still rolling around, sneezing. The other three were worrying the two remaining hunters.

Rory arrived just as the hunters pulled over a shelving unit. It landed on top of one of their attackers, pinning it down. The other Desponds appeared to share their fellow's distress. They shied away from the men who had caused it.

The hunters seized their chance to rescue their fallen friend. They made for the front door, carrying him between them. The Desponds watched them go, but didn't follow.

They sniffed the air, sensing a better prospect.

The Desponds turned on Rory. They were between him and the front door. The fire exit was too far away for him to reach before they caught him.

Rory backed up to the window, even as Mr Henry slammed the steel shutter down over it. He tried to lift the shutter from this side, but it had locked into place.

Rory hammered on the shutter. He shouted for someone to let him out. No one came. He was trapped. Trapped in here with four hungry Desponds.

Two of which were advancing upon Rory, slavering and licking their lips.

Typical, thought Rory. *I rushed in here to save someone else, and now I'm the one who needs saving!*

The safe-cracker pinged. It had found the security code for the spaceport computers.

"Awaiting instructions," said the read-out screen.

The Doctor stood up. He returned the repaired sonic screwdriver to his pocket. 'Hello again, computer,' he said. 'This is your alien infestation speaking. And yes, I do have some instructions for you. Since you asked.'

The Doctor flexed his fingers, eagerly.

Oh no, thought Janie. Everything had been going so well! Almost all of the passengers, staff and flight crew in the spaceport had been checked in. Only four people were missing, and a group of volunteers had gone in search of them.

And then, a walking stick had come flying through the duty-free shop window. It had been followed, a moment later, by Mr Henry — and then by his wife and Rory.

The passengers didn't know what was happening. Some of them were drawn to the shop to find out; others ran as far away from it as they could.

And, as the passengers ran, the Desponds began to stir again.

Janie could see five of them. No, six. They were lurking in the corners of the departure lounge, just watching... for now.

Other people saw the Desponds too, and they froze or backed away or just sank to their knees. It had been their raised hopes that had been warding off the Desponds. No longer. With every passenger that gave in to fear or despair, the creatures grew bolder. They stood a little bit taller. They drew a little bit closer.

Janie dropped her clipboard and sat down with a sigh. It was her own fault, she supposed, for believing in the Doctor. She ought to have known better.

She shouldn't have got her hopes up.

Then, someone shouted, 'Look!' He pointed up at the monitors above their heads – and all the passengers looked.

The departure boards were updating.

Janie didn't know what it meant, at first. She only saw that the list of endlessly delayed flights – a list that hadn't changed in five long months – was gone. In its place, only three flights were listed – but next to each of those flights were two magic words. Two words that Janie hadn't seen in what felt like forever:Now Boarding.

He had done it, Janie realised. He had actually done it. The Doctor had kept his word. The quarantine of Spaceport Terminal 4000 was over!

CHAPTER 16
FLIGHTS NOW BOARDING

'What's everyone standing around for?'

Janie recognised the Doctor's voice. She shook herself. She had been staring at the departure boards for at least a minute, hardly able to believe her eyes.

Not that she was the only one.

She remembered the Desponds. She looked for them, but most of them had gone. She saw the back end of one as it retreated into the first-class lounge.

The renewed hopes of the passengers had repelled the creatures again.

'I said, why is everyone standing around?' The

Doctor strode into the centre of the crowd. 'I thought you all had flights to catch.'

That got their attention. Within seconds, the departure lounge was a hive of activity once more. Janie found herself at the heart of it. Everyone wanted to be sure their names were on her list. They wanted to know which ship they were leaving on.

Rory stepped out of the duty-free shop. He wrestled the faulty sliding door shut. He looked around, bewildered.

Everything was as it had been before. Even the Henrys were acting as if nothing had happened. Queues were forming at the airlock doors for the docked ships, and the Henrys had joined one of these.

The Doctor was here. He had just collared a pair of security guards. 'First-class lounge,' he said. 'There's a Despond in there. If you're quick, you can board it in.'

'We, ah, trapped four more,' said Rory, 'in the shop.'

'Yeah, I saw,' said the Doctor, 'on the cameras. Shame you almost caused a panic in the process. Classic Rory!'

'Hey,' said Rory, 'you're the one who got yourself bitten. I'm just saying.'

The Doctor was making his way along the departure lounge, stopping to peer through each porthole in turn. 'Aren't you going to ask?' he said.

Rory hurried to keep up with him. 'Aren't I going to ask what?'

'How you got out of there. Last thing I saw, you were backed up against a shutter with two Desponds eyeing up your throat.'

'They just sort of backed off,' said Rory. 'You did that, I suppose?'

'I rekindled the passengers' hopes,' said the Doctor. 'And, as there was a crowd of passengers outside the shop…'

Rory understood. 'The Desponds could sense them, even through the shutter. Like before. There was too much hope for them. Doctor, what are you doing?'

'I'm looking for something.'

'Out there? In space?'

'Out there.' The Doctor came to a halt. He pointed through a porthole. 'In space.'

Rory followed the Doctor's finger. He felt his stomach sinking. He could see a familiar object, drifting against the stars. It was the TARDIS.

Amy rotated the view on the TARDIS's scanner screen. At first, she could see only space. Then, a large, white spinning-top shape came into view.

The spaceport! Amy could almost have cried with relief.

'No! I won't go back there! You can't make me go back there!'

She had forgotten that Roger was behind her. The fight had quite gone out of him, though. He was more despairing than desperate.

'We aren't going anywhere,' said Amy, 'thanks to you. We're adrift in space and I don't know how to get us back. So, you just… behave!'

At least the TARDIS hadn't gone far, thought

Amy, as she turned back to the scanner screen. She just hoped that the Doctor could find it out here.

'What do we do?' asked Rory.

'I don't know,' said the Doctor. 'It depends.'

'Depends on what?'

'On who's at the TARDIS controls right now. Have you seen Amy lately?'

'I thought she… you mean she might be…?'

'Could have been worse,' said the Doctor. 'At least I remembered the handbrake.'

'The handbrake?' Rory echoed.

'It's a bit worn,' the Doctor confessed. 'Still. Should keep the TARDIS within about a mile or so of here, and with minimal time slippage.'

He was rifling through his pockets. He unearthed a toothbrush, a ball of string and a clockwork frog, all of which he offloaded onto Rory.

'Of course, if we could find a spacesuit…'

'I'm not doing another spacewalk,' said Rory. 'No way!'

'I seem to have lost my door key, anyway.' The Doctor produced a white plastic card triumphantly.

'Galactic Express!' he said. 'Never leave home without it. Tell you what, Rory, I'll deal with the TARDIS – you stop that fight.'

'What fight?'

'The one about to break out behind me.' The Doctor pointed over his shoulder.

Mr and Mrs Henry were arguing with a pair of flight attendants.

Janie had rushed onto the scene. She was doing her best to calm things down, but Mr Henry was getting more angry. He was pointing with his walking stick.

A few more passengers were crowding around too, joining in the debate.

Rory groaned. 'Now what?'

The Doctor didn't answer him.

He had spied a row of payphones by the wall. He ran towards them. He snatched up one of the phones, swiped his card through a reader and began to dial.

'I'm sorry,' said Roger.

Amy turned to him, surprised. He was slumped on a step. 'You what?'

'I said I'm sorry, okay?' he snapped. 'I suppose I got a little... frantic.'

Amy grimaced. 'You think?'

'You don't know what it's been like for me,' said Roger. 'You've been here all of five minutes. For me, it's been five months!'

'You're not the only one,' said Amy.

'I know. But I was... I was scared, okay? I saw what those monsters, the Desponds, did to people, and –'

'They never fed on you?'

'I never let them,' said Roger. 'The nearest they got... it was back at the beginning. I still had my gun. Two of them came at me. I panicked.'

'That was when you shot a Despond?'

'Right between the eyes,' said Roger. 'I also shot two plates in the food court, took out a light fitting and grazed a passenger on the arm.'

He buried his face in his hands. 'Five months I've spent, keeping out of their way. I've been jumping at shadows, sleeping with one eye open. I… I've done things I'm not proud of. And where has it got me? I've no hope left, anyway.'

'It'll work this time,' Amy promised him. 'The Doctor will fix this.'

Roger shrugged. 'He can't fix things for me. If I get on one of those spaceships with the others, I'll just be swapping one prison for another.'

'What do you mean?'

'I mean, they'll lock me up for sure. It's my fault, you see. It's all my fault. I let the Desponds loose in the spaceport.'

Roger looked up at Amy. He was expecting some reaction.

She had hardly even heard him. Something else had caught her attention.

'Do you hear that?' asked Amy. 'Do you hear that sound?'

The TARDIS telephone was ringing.

The row in the departure lounge had escalated.

The Henrys had started it, of course. According to a stressed Janie, they had reacted badly when told they would be in the second group to board their ship. They had refused to leave the queue in which they stood.

This had sparked an avalanche of appeals from the other passengers.

'...been here longer than any of...'

'...those of us who trapped the Desponds should surely get to...'

'...paid good money for a first-class ticket, which I think entitles me to...'

Janie stood firm against these unreasonable demands. She insisted that everyone would just have to wait their turn.

So, the passengers turned to Rory, as 'the Doctor's friend', to overrule her.

They were tugging at his sleeve, shouting in his ear. He couldn't possibly answer all their pleas at once.

One man pressed money into Rory's hand, trying to bribe him. Another was begging for his sick grandmother to be moved up the passenger lists.

An elegant-looking woman was complaining in shrill tones about the ship to which she had been assigned… and in fact, Rory realised, she was talking about Cap's beaten-up old charter ship, so he could hardly blame her.

He didn't know what to say to any of them.

So, the passengers were giving up on Rory now, too. They were turning on each other instead, yelling and jabbing fingers.

The Doctor had been right. This was about to turn into another fight.

Rory jumped up onto a chair. 'Please,' he said, 'if everyone could just… this isn't getting us…' No one was listening to him.

'*Quiet!*' Rory yelled.

A hush fell over the crowd. They all stared up at Rory, surprised by the authority in his voice. He had surprised himself too.

'The Doctor put Janie in charge of this evacuation,' he continued. 'So, if you lot can't listen to her and… and do as she says, then no one will be going anywhere.'

Too much, he thought. He had sounded a bit petulant. In fact, he had sounded like his old Year 7 schoolteacher.

Rory's outburst had had an effect, though. The passengers were doing as he said. Even Mr and Mrs Henry were returning to their seats, though not without a few final grumbles. Janie and the other flight attendants took over, and soon they had three orderly queues stretching along the departure lounge.

All quarrels were forgotten, then. A thrill of anticipation hung in the air as the flight attendants opened the airlock doors and the passengers began to file onto the waiting spaceships. *It's working,* thought Rory. *This is actually working!*

He glanced over at the Doctor. He was still on the phone, talking animatedly.

Then, Rory heard a scream.

Mr Henry leapt to his feet. 'I knew it!' he bellowed. 'I knew this would happen!'

The Desponds were back.

They were coming from all directions: six of them. They were barking and snapping, and foaming at the mouths. Rory had never seen them so worked up before.

The Desponds fell upon the passengers, and all hell broke loose.

CHAPTER 17
A DESPERATE BATTLE

Amy dashed around the console room with a phone tucked under her chin. She was following instructions from the Doctor.

'*Now,*' said the Doctor, '*disengage the temporal dislocation combobulator.*'

'The what?'

'*Looks like the front panel of a clock radio. Second button from the left.*'

'Yeah, I see it. Gonna have to put the phone down.'

Amy left the phone hanging by its cord, from its cradle in the console.

She found the control that the Doctor had

described. 'Well, that actually is a bit of an old clock radio,' she muttered. She hit the 'snooze' button.

She picked up the phone again. 'What now?'

'*Now,*' said the Doctor, '*I have to go. Despond trouble!*'

'But…'

'*I'm going to need you to do one more thing for me. Stay on the line, Amy. When I give you the word, you need to pull the big lever. The one to your left now. But not before I give the word. That's important, Amy. The timing has to be spot on.*'

'What's happening there?' asked Amy. 'Doctor?'

But the Doctor had gone.

Amy looked across the console at Roger. He was still sitting on the steps. He returned her gaze with a helpless shrug.

Amy pressed the TARDIS phone to her ear. Was it her imagination, or could she hear people screaming?

The departure lounge was in chaos.

Everyone was shouting and running. They were

fighting each other – and the flight attendants – to reach the airlocks, or just panicking and heading for cover.

Rory found himself lost in the confusion. He had already seen three people fed upon. It didn't make any sense! The passengers had been in their highest hopes yet. Shouldn't that have kept the Desponds at bay?

He fought his way through the scrum. He found himself next to Mr and Mrs Henry. Mr Henry grabbed Rory by the front of his shirt.

'Do you see what you've done?' he roared. 'You and your friends?'

'We had all we needed,' Mrs Henry wailed. 'Our own two rows of chairs, with our coats and towels to sleep under and the washrooms across the way.'

'We said the Desponds wouldn't let us go. We told you so.'

'Mr Henry is right. You should have listened to him.'

'They'll feed on us all now,' said Mr Henry. 'The Desponds will drain us all dry!'

Rory didn't know what to say. Before he could say anything, someone ran into him from behind. He was sent flying. He grabbed hold of Mrs Henry to steady himself. Mrs Henry shrieked and shoved him away from her.

A Despond had appeared behind Rory. It was snarling and spitting.

Rory backed away slowly. He collided with a group of people who were backing away from a Despond of their own.

The creatures went for their nearest targets. They snapped at their legs, with their normal mouths. As far as Rory could see, they weren't using their feeding tentacles.

The Henrys were right, he realised. The Desponds were more intelligent than Rory had supposed. They had eaten enough – but they saw that people were leaving the spaceport, and they were desperate to stop them.

They didn't want to lose their food source.

Rory picked up a chair. He prodded a Despond with it, until it let its victim go. The Despond rounded on Rory instead. It leapt at him, and now its feeding tentacle *was* extended! Rory threw the chair at it. Chair and Despond collided in mid-air, and both dropped to the floor. The Despond got tangled up in the chair legs.

The flight attendants were trying to close the airlock doors, before the Desponds could squeeze through them. If they got onto a spaceship, and fed on the flight crew…

It didn't even bear thinking about.

Rory stumbled over a body. It was a woman, one of those who had been fed on. She was curled up into a ball, sobbing.

As Rory's hand brushed the floor, a Despond leapt at him. It clamped its jaws around his arm. He tried to shake it off, but its grip was too strong.

The creature's teeth sank into his flesh. Rory extended two fingers and thrust them towards the Despond's eyes. The Despond flinched before his fingers could reach it. It let go of Rory's arm and ran off.

Rory felt a hand on his shoulder. He turned.

The Doctor had found him.

'Doctor,' he gasped. 'The Desponds. They –'

'Yeah. I can see that for myself,' said the Doctor. 'I thought this might happen.'

'You did? Great. Thanks for, y'know, the warning.'

'I have a plan,' said the Doctor, 'but you might not like it.'

'I like it,' said Rory. 'Any plan right now. Anything.'

The Doctor held up the sonic screwdriver. He pushed a button on its side.

'And especially,' said Rory, 'any plan that involves sonicking. You're making that sound, right? The one that no one can hear, but it repels the Desponds?'

'Um, not quite,' said the Doctor.

'What does "not quite" mean?'

'Never did find that frequency,' said the Doctor. 'Amy did, but she never got around to showing me. So, this is the other one.'

'The other what? Oh, no! You don't mean the other –?'

'The other frequency,' the Doctor confirmed. 'The one I found by accident when we first got here. The one that, um, attracts them.'

Rory could hear the Desponds howling in anguish. The howls were growing closer.

Now he could see them, too. They were pushing their way through the crowd, ignoring everyone else in their need to find the source of their pain.

Every Despond in the spaceport was closing in on the Doctor and Rory.

'I found them in a cargo ship hold,' said Roger.

Amy was hanging on the TARDIS phone. She didn't really want to talk – but it seemed that Roger had to get this off his chest.

'It was a routine security check,' he explained. 'The mother must have snuck aboard at the last port of call. She had died giving birth to her litter.'

'The Desponds?' guessed Amy.

'Thirteen of them. Thirteen little puppies. According to regulations, I should have had them destroyed.'

'No.'

'I couldn't bring myself… there's a storeroom down by the power plant, where no one ever goes. I hid them in there. I looked after them. They ate real food, back then. The first time a Despond went for my throat, I thought it was just being playful.'

'What happened?' asked Amy.

'They grew up,' said Roger. 'They developed those feeding tentacles. I… I didn't know what to do. Then, one of the other guards, a friend of mine… I think she must have heard them whining. She opened the storeroom door.'

'The Desponds got out into the spaceport,' concluded Amy.

'And that triggered the automatic quarantine,' said Roger.

He stood up. He approached Amy again. She was ready in case he tried anything.

'Does the Doctor really have a plan?' asked Roger. 'Can he really end this?'

'I… I don't know,' said Amy. 'I was waiting for

his word, but…' She looked down at the phone. 'I can't hear a thing. I think we might have been cut off.'

'How many Desponds do you count?' asked the Doctor.

'Five,' said Rory, nervously. 'No, six.'

'Plus four in the duty-free shop, one in the first-class lounge, one dead in Space Traffic Control… That'll be the lot, then.'

The Doctor and Rory backed away from the advancing Desponds. They were nearing the end of the departure lounge.

'Remember what I said about liking this plan?' said Rory. 'I've gone off it.'

'It's working, though,' said the Doctor. He waggled the sonic screwdriver. The Desponds' eyes followed it, as if they were hypnotised.

Behind them, Janie had reopened the airlock doors and was hurrying the passengers through them. 'A couple of minutes more,' said the Doctor, 'and everyone will be safely out of here. Well, everyone but us. Here, catch!'

He tossed the sonic screwdriver Rory's way. Rory almost dropped it. 'Keep the button pressed down,' said the Doctor. He darted over to the side of the duty-free shop to grab something. A red fire extinguisher.

The Doctor shook the extinguisher. It was empty. He dropped it, and grabbed another. At the same time, two Desponds charged at Rory.

The Doctor jumped into their path and blasted them with extinguisher foam.

The Desponds spluttered and fell back – but Rory could see two more, sneaking up around him from opposite sides. The Doctor blasted one of them. Rory vaulted a row of red plastic chairs to escape the other.

The Despond squeezed under a chair to reach him. It yelped as a jet of freezing cold foam struck it up the rear end.

Rory scrambled over the chairs to rejoin the Doctor. They backed up to the wall as the Desponds advanced upon them again. The

Doctor took the sonic screwdriver back and gave the extinguisher to Rory. He sprayed it in a wide arc in front of him.

'There'd better be another part to this plan,' said Rory.

He hadn't noticed the row of payphones behind them.

The Doctor had left a phone off the hook. He snatched it up now, and shouted into the handset: 'Now, Amy! The lever! Amy… Amy, are you there?'

The Doctor fumbled through his pockets. He found his white plastic card and swiped it through the reader, three times. His face fell.

'What? What is it?' asked Rory.

'Out of credit,' said the Doctor.

'And that's bad, right?'

'That's bad.' The Doctor let go of the phone. 'Because, if I can't get a message to Amy…' He didn't have to finish the sentence.

The six Desponds were straining ever further forward, as if sensing the weakness of their cornered prey. The fire extinguisher sputtered in

Rory's hands, about to run dry.

'You were right,' said the Doctor. 'This was a bad plan. A very, very bad plan.'

CHAPTER 18
DEPARTURES

'So, this is it,' said Rory.

'Looks like it,' the Doctor agreed.

'This is where I'm going to live out the rest of my days. In Terminal 4000.'

'Yup.'

'I'll never think about leaving, even though I can see the TARDIS right outside the window. Even though I know my wife is in there.'

'That's about the size of it.'

'Because the Desponds will have sucked every last drop of hope out of me.'

'There is a bright side,' said the Doctor. 'Two bright sides, in fact.'

He looked along the departure lounge. The spaceships had finished boarding. Cap's charter ship had disengaged its locking clamps and was already pulling away.

The evacuation was complete. The stranded passengers had escaped.

'And the other bright side?' asked Rory.

He still had the fire extinguisher. He was aiming it more selectively now, to preserve its contents. Even so, the white foam was coming out in fits and starts.

'There's no food,' said the Doctor. 'So, "the rest of our days" won't be all that long.'

The extinguisher was completely empty. Rory threw it at the Desponds. The gesture bought them about half a second.

Then the six Desponds charged forward.

Amy had hung up the TARDIS phone. She glared at it as if sheer willpower could make it ring again.

'The Doctor gave you instructions?' asked Roger.

'Yeah, he told me what to do,' said Amy, 'just

not when. He said the timing was important.' Her hand went to the big lever by the phone. She hesitated.

'You should do it,' said Roger.

'But what if I time it wrong? What if I should have waited longer?'

'What if you wait too long?' Roger pointed to the scanner screen. 'Look!'

Amy looked up. 'The ships,' she breathed. 'They're leaving!'

'The Doctor did it,' said Roger.

'He did,' agreed Amy. 'Maybe that's why he never came back to the phone. Maybe the Doctor and Rory are on one of those ships, and they don't need this after all.'

She looked at the lever, doubtfully.

'Or not,' she said. 'I don't know. What... what do you think?'

'I think you've got to have hope,' said Roger.

Amy looked at him, surprised. He was right, of course. She just hadn't expected him to be the one to say it.

She nodded. Roger held up his hand. He had crossed his fingers for her.

Amy closed her eyes. She drew in a deep breath. She pulled the lever.

The first Despond leapt at Rory's throat. He managed to bat it away, but the second was right behind it.

The Doctor was under attack too. The other creatures had closed in around their prey, keeping the two of them contained. There was nowhere to run.

Then Rory heard a familiar sound. A wheezing, groaning sound.

A blue haze appeared in the air between him and the six Desponds.

The sound grew louder, and the blue haze thicker. A springing Despond was flung back in mid-air by some invisible force.

Then, Rory could see the dog-like creatures no longer. The spaceport was gone too. He was standing inside the TARDIS, by the console. The Doctor was still beside him. So was Amy, and –

Rory did a double-take at this – Roger.

The Doctor turned to Amy. 'I thought I told you to wait for my cue,' he said. Then a grin broke out on his face. 'Good job you didn't, though.'

'Good to see you too,' said Amy.

The Doctor ran around the console, operating it with his usual manic energy.

'I don't get it,' said Rory. 'What happened?'

'What happened was,' the Doctor explained, 'Amy here – clever, wonderful Amy – just flew the TARDIS. Not only that, but her timing was perfect.'

'I think…' said Amy. 'Did I just land the TARDIS *around* the two of you?'

Rory noticed the scanner screen. It was showing an image of the spaceport departure lounge. It was empty now, but for the six Desponds.

They were howling and whimpering. A couple lay on their sides, whining pitifully to themselves. Rory almost felt sorry for the creatures. They had lost all hope.

'That reminds me.' The Doctor gestured across the console. 'Amy. The temporal dislocation combobulator. You need to turn it back on.'

'Got it,' said Amy.

'While you're there, you could give the helmic regulator a quick boost and crank up the thermo buffer. Rory? You could… well, you could put the kettle on. Or something. Oh, and Roger… was that your name?'

Roger straightened up, surprised. He started towards the Doctor.

The Doctor held up a hand to stop him. 'Don't you even talk to me!'

'What are you doing?' asked Rory.

The TARDIS was taking off. The sound of its engines filled the console room. The image on the scanner screen had disintegrated into static.

'Concentrating,' said the Doctor. 'This next part is a bit tricky. I'm going to land the TARDIS inside a moving vehicle.'

The Doctor stepped out of the TARDIS. He was greeted once again by cheers and applause. 'You know,' he said to Amy and Rory, 'I could get quite used to this.'

They had landed aboard a spaceship. It was filled with passengers from the spaceport terminal. They were sitting in rows, all buckled in. They were nibbling on stale pretzels, which the flight attendants must have found and distributed.

Rory recognised two of them. 'Mr and Mrs Henry,' he said. 'I'm glad you made it.'

The Henrys shushed him crossly, waving him aside. He was blocking their view of the in-flight movie. Rory scowled at the couple as he moved.

A flight attendant appeared from the cockpit. 'Doctor!' she cried, joyfully.

'Janie Collins!' cried the Doctor, as Janie flung her arms around him. 'Looking a bit more cheerful.'

'Thanks to you,' said Janie.

'How about the rest of them? Did everyone make it out?'

Janie noticed Roger hovering in the TARDIS doorway.

'They have now,' she said. 'Ours was the last

ship to leave. We've radioed the other two, and everything is okay with them. A few problems with the charter ship – with its owner, more than anything – but nothing we need to worry about.'

'Where will you go?' asked Amy.

'Terminal 3999, and onward flights from there,' said Janie. 'Estimated flight time is about thirty and a half hours.'

'Thirty and a half hours?' The Doctor's jaw dropped open in horror.

Amy elbowed him in the ribs. 'Behave,' she hissed. 'Remember. We can't all go whizzing about the universe in a super-duper police box.'

'I need you to do one more thing for me,' said the Doctor to Janie.

'Anything,' she said.

'Take care of the Desponds. Yeah, I know that sounds mad after all they did to you. I know how they hurt you, but –'

'But it wasn't their fault,' said Janie. 'They just acted according to their nature.'

The Doctor grinned. 'I knew you'd understand.'

'And they're like us now, aren't they? I mean, they're like we used to be. They're stranded at Terminal 4000, like we were stranded. And they have no food.'

'Here,' said the Doctor. He showed Janie his psychic paper. Anyone who saw that paper saw what the Doctor wanted them to see.

'Details of an animal welfare organisation,' he said. 'An alien animal welfare organisation. They'll know what to do with the Desponds.'

'I'll contact them as soon as I can,' Janie promised.

Roger had slipped away. He found himself a seat towards the back of the passenger cabin. He looked surprised as Amy sat down beside him.

'I know what you're thinking,' she said.

'I don't know what to do,' said Roger. 'There's bound to be an enquiry. Do I tell them the truth about the Desponds or…?'

'You can't take all the blame,' said Amy. 'You tried to do a good thing. I mean, yeah, you broke a few silly rules, but –'

'This'll cost the spaceport company billions in payouts. Mr and Mrs Henry have asked for the forms already. They'll be looking for someone to blame.'

'You couldn't have known all this would happen,' said Amy. 'Anyway, that company of yours have a lot to answer for too – leaving you all stranded.'

'Your husband's looking over here.'

Roger was right. Rory was giving him the evil eye.

'Don't mind him,' said Amy. 'He doesn't like it when I talk to other men.'

'Um, yeah,' said Roger. 'And I did... when I lost my mind for a bit, back there, I did kind of... I knocked him out. And then I threw him out of an airlock.'

'You did what?'

'Will you tell him I'm sorry?'

'Yeah, you know what?' said Amy. 'I think you should tell the truth to that enquiry, after all. Tell them the whole story. I'm sure they'll be every bit as forgiving as I am.'

They didn't stay long. The Doctor hated goodbyes. So, as soon as he knew he wasn't needed any more, he ushered Amy and Rory back into the TARDIS.

'Random coordinates,' he decided. 'And let's hope we end up somewhere more interesting than a spaceport... okay, more interesting than *most* spaceports.'

'They will be all right, won't they?' said Amy.

'Who?' The Doctor looked up from the console as if he had forgotten already.

'The passengers. Janie. What the Desponds did to them...'

'Worn off already, in most cases. They might have a few bad dreams, but otherwise no lasting effects. Well, look at me: I'm as fit as a flea.'

The Doctor ran up and down on the spot to prove his point.

'That's "a fiddle",' said Rory. 'It's "as fit as a fiddle".'

'Are you sure?' said the Doctor. 'I always thought it was "a flea". Anyway, don't worry about the former residents of Spaceport Terminal 4000. It's like you said before, Amy. Hope's an inexhaustible commodity. No matter how bad things might sometimes seem, there's always hope.'

THE END

DOCTOR WHO

THE WEB IN SPACE

DAVID BAILEY

CHAPTER 1
RINGTONES

Imagine a quiet little corner of the galaxy where nothing ever happens.

No silver space liners ever glide by, showing their awestruck passengers the wondrous delights of the astral wilds. Because there's nothing here but a heap of spinning rocks.

No military ships ever come here, their hulls bristling with laser cannons and neutron torpedoes, bravely patrolling the spaceways. There are never any wars here, because there's nothing worth fighting over.

Even if you got lost while piloting your spaceship, you'd have to get *very* lost to find this place. It's so far from anywhere else. The Gloriana Scattering is an out-of-the-way asteroid field, just a vast expanse of giant rocks, light years from end to end. There's nothing remarkable about this place whatsoever.

No signs of life, nothing at all.

Usually.

Today, however, the captain of one ship has decided to take a shortcut through the Gloriana Scattering – and that is the biggest mistake she will ever make…

Amy clamped her palms over her ears, but it made no difference. The TARDIS control room was trembling to the noise of a deep, honking siren. The sound was like a foghorn. A *loud* foghorn. Amy was sure it was shaking the teeth out of her head!

It was things like this that often made Amy wonder who on earth had designed these time machines. But then that was the point – TARDISes *weren't* designed on Earth. Were they even designed at all? Amy remembered the Doctor had once said something about *growing* new TARDISes. Well, however they came into being, they were clearly meant for aliens with odd ideas about emergency sirens and really terrible hearing!

'Should it be making that noise?' she yelled.

The Doctor ignored her. He was whirling around the console, flicking switches, pushing buttons and saying 'Oops!' a lot.

Rory staggered down the stairway to join them. 'I was asleep!' he shouted at Amy.

'I booked an alarm call for you,' she replied.

'What? I can't hear you!'

'I booked an alarm call!'

'*You* did this?' Rory looked appalled.

'Oh, don't be so stupid!' Amy realised she shouldn't try to crack jokes at anything higher than eighty decibels.

The Doctor suddenly stopped dancing in circles, and leant in between his two friends. '*You* did this, Amelia!' He had to shout over the cacophony. She blinked, and was sure she felt her hair move in the rush of air caused by the Doctor's bellowing.

'Wait, what? How did I do this?'

The Doctor pointed at a row of round, black buttons – they were like the keys of an old-fashioned typewriter. One of them was pressed down and illuminated with a little green light. 'Remember those?'

'What? No. They're just buttons!'

Rory was standing right next to Amy now. He shouted into her ear, 'You *did* do this, then?'

'Rory! Doctor! I didn't do anything!'

The thundering foghorn blared on, louder and louder.

'Ringtones!' the Doctor yelled. He reached for a small rubber-headed hammer that hung on a hook on the edge of the console. He took it, then – thump! He smacked the row of buttons, the little green light flickered out… and the siren shut down. The manic hooting sound didn't stop straight away. It slowly ran out of steam, first honking more slowly, then honking more quietly – until it stopped with a weak little 'ppplllrb' noise.

'Ringtones,' he said again, returning to his busy

work at the console.

'What about ringtones?' Amy jogged around the console, trying to keep up with the Time Lord.

'You wanted to change the TARDIS's ringtone, I told you which buttons to press.' The Doctor waved a hand towards the row of now battered-looking buttons. 'And now look. Someone wants to phone me, and we get that racket!'

Rory laughed. 'That was the phone?'

'Well,' Amy said, 'aren't you going to answer it?'

The Doctor stopped what he was doing. 'It's not ringing.' He gazed at the column of glass above the console. Rising and falling, rising and falling. He was lost in his own thoughts.

'Well, no, it's not ringing *now*,' sighed Amy. 'You smashed the controls with a hammer!'

'What?' He snapped out of his daze, looking first at Amy, then at the row of buttons. 'Oh, that! No, they're just the ultrasonic influx hinges. We don't need them.'

Amy glared at him. 'Then what was all that stuff about ringtones?'

'Oh, they do that as well – but that wasn't the *phone*.' The Doctor looked bewildered at Amy's question. 'What phone sounds like that?'

Amy shook her head in disbelief. The Doctor could be so infuriating sometimes!

'That was a distress signal,' he continued, 'calling to the TARDIS via the influx hinges. But the old girl got her wires crossed.' The Doctor gently patted the console. 'She sounded the ringtone, not the emergency alarm.'

Amy rubbed her brow. Her head was starting to hurt. 'So, that was the phone ringing?'

'It was the *sound* of the phone ringing.' The Doctor had that explaining-things-to-idiots thing going on with his voice. 'But it was *actually* the emergency alarm.'

Rory cleared his throat, opened his mouth to ask a question – but then obviously thought better of it.

'If that was the phone ringing instead of the alarm,' said Amy, slowly, 'then what does the real alarm sound like?'

The Doctor awkwardly leant over the buttons, peering closely at them. 'Ah! You know that noise water makes when it goes down a plughole? All shlurpy and swirly?'

'Yes?'

'Nothing like that.'

Just then, there was a soft chime and the glass column slid to a halt. The background hum of the TARDIS changed slightly, growing quieter as the engines powered down. The Doctor sprang away from the console, grinning from ear to ear. 'And here we are!'

'I swear, I'll never get used to this,' Rory muttered to himself. He then raised his voice and asked the Doctor, 'So, where is "here"?'

'Did you miss the bit where I said "distress signal"? We're right where the signal came from…'

The Doctor stepped out of the TARDIS – and walked into a line of guns, all pointed straight at him. A line of men and women were facing him. They were all dressed in grey jumpsuits with black pads on their knees and elbows. They wore tough-looking black coverings on their heads, like motorcycle helmets without visors.

The Doctor raised his hands quickly. 'Hello! Nice to meet you,' he said.

Amy and Rory barrelled into the Doctor's back, and the three of them tumbled out of their time machine's doorway. They had materialised in a long, white corridor. The walls were made of glossy white plastic, and the floor was shiny and white, too. Little red lights were flashing all the way along the corridor, and a siren – a lot quieter than the one in the TARDIS – was echoing through the air.

One of the guards, a short young man with messy blonde hair poking out from under his helmet, stepped forward. He looked nervous – the Doctor could see a sheen of sweat glistening on his forehead, and his blue eyes were wide with fear. He raised his gun higher, pointing it straight at the Doctor's left heart. 'We won't let you get away with this,' he stammered. 'Captain Jones will not allow her cargo to be stolen.'

'What cargo?' Rory said. 'We're not going to steal anything!'

'We've come in response to your distress signal,' the Doctor said again. 'And I don't mean to sound rude, but we're your rescuers and you don't seem terribly grateful...'

'Doctor,' Amy hissed, shutting him up. She turned to the line of soldiers. 'I'm sorry about him, he's got no manners. I'm Amy, this is the Doctor, and that's Rory. We're here to help you.' She smiled and held out her open hands in a friendly gesture.

The young man thought for a second, then lowered his weapon. 'I'm Ensign Sam Appleseed,' he said. 'Technical officer, second class, aboard the ECC ship *Black Horizon*.'

The other soldiers seemed to relax a little, too. Good old Amy could always put strangers at their ease. The Doctor wondered why people didn't respond to him in quite the same way. Did he look odd? Something about the jacket? The hair? Whatever it was, it couldn't be the bow tie...

The Doctor's thoughts were interrupted by a crackle of static and a series of electronic bleeps. 'What's that?' he asked.

Sam, now looking more worried than before, shushed the Doctor and whispered, 'Listen!'

A voice rang out along the corridor, broadcast on a series of loudspeakers hanging from the ceiling. 'Prepare to be boarded,' it said, in a cold, harsh robotic tone. 'You will surrender your technology!'

Sam turned to his fellow guards. They looked all around themselves, as if worried they'd be attacked at any moment.

'Ah, I see,' said the Doctor in a slow drawl. 'He said, "Prepare to be boarded." This is a spaceship, is that right?'

Sam nodded.

'And you're under attack from some sort of...'

'We don't know exactly who is attacking us, Doctor,' Sam replied.

'Doesn't matter,' the Doctor said, waving his hand dismissively in the air. 'We can figure that out later. What I want to know is this: why aren't your engines running? Because that's a pretty important thing for a spaceship – got to keep the engines running, or you won't *go* anywhere. And if you're under attack, you'd think a spaceship would want to move *away* from the attackers. But I can't hear engines. Amy! Can you hear engines?'

Amy just shrugged, shaking her head.

'Rory!' the Doctor barked, spinning to face his other companion. 'Can *you* hear engines?'

'I'm not sure what engines sound like,' he replied.

'You know, like vroom! Or swoosh! Or – at the very least, if you're inside a big old spaceship like this – a kind of deep, low rumble…' The Doctor looked all around the corridor. He looked up at the ceiling, down at the floor. He leapt over to the wall and crammed his ear against the white plastic surface. 'But I can't hear a thing. This ship is silent.'

'I think I should take you to Captain Jones,' Sam said at last. 'She can explain things better than I can…'

CHAPTER 2
BREAKDOWN

Although she wore exactly the same black-and-grey uniform as her crew, Captain Jones was easy to spot. She stood at the highest point of the control room, on a platform raised above all the consoles and workstations, like a queen surveying her realm. She wasn't all that tall, but she stood stiffly upright, her chin jutting out with pride and authority. Her chestnut-coloured hair hung to her shoulders. Amy thought it looked a little untidy, like it hadn't been cut in some time – but she supposed that the captain of a spaceship had more to worry about than her hair.

As the Doctor and his friends walked into the

room, the captain glanced briefly in their direction with a frown, then turned her attention to the giant viewscreen which took up one wall of the room. Her brown eyes looked tired, ringed with red.

'Situation?' she said, her voice clipped and clear.

As one of her crew started to read off a list of numbers and readings, Rory stared at the viewscreen. The screen was filled with grey, ragged rocks, all turning and tumbling through space. The ship seemed to be stuck in an asteroid field. A scattering of stars was visible in the background, and one larger sun hung much closer to the asteroids, spilling its light across the view.

'The Gloriana Scattering,' the Doctor sighed, a dreamy smile spreading across his face. 'One of the most beautiful asteroid fields in the universe. If you like rocks, that is. And I do. I *do* like a good rock.'

'You're weird,' Amy said.

'Indeed I am,' the Doctor said, not really paying any attention. 'And look at that! That star there, Gloriana XVI. All its planets blown to pieces in a gravity quake, thousands of years ago. That's what the asteroid field is – the poor, shattered remains of Gloriana's children.'

Normally, Rory was willing to listen to every word of the Doctor's wittering – there was often something worth hearing in among all the chatter! But this time, he had stopped paying attention a few words in. He had spotted something on the viewscreen, slowly weaving its way through the dangerously spinning rocks.

He had seen a spaceship.

In his travels with the Doctor, Rory had seen quite a few spaceships. He remembered that fantastic night at Stonehenge, when the sky had been full of them. All shapes and sizes, made from all sorts of metals and plastics and who knew what else. But this ship – the one slowly working its way towards the *Black Horizon*... this ship was different.

Rory squinted at it. He had to stop himself from laughing. It looked ridiculous!

The spaceship had seven wings, or fins, or

somethings… half of its back end looked like the tail on a cartoon rocket, all sleek curves and shining silver. The other half looked like a misshapen lump of melted plastic. It had two engines on one side, and none at the back. Aerials and antennae and radar dishes were dotted all over its surface, pointing in every direction. Its hull was metal, but bumpy and dented, like it had been ripped from one ship and wrapped around this one. It looked like crumpled tinfoil.

No one bit of the ship looked like another. It was a patchwork spaceship.

'Well,' gasped the Doctor, 'would you look at that?' He strode confidently into the centre of the control room and gazed up at the viewscreen.

Amy and Rory walked to his side. 'What is it?' asked Rory. 'It looks like a flying scrapheap!'

'Oh, I wouldn't say that, Rory!' The Doctor started to point out the different parts of the approaching spaceship. 'That's the hull plating from a Dalek saucer. And that's the engine from a Sontaran warsphere! Oh, and look at that, that's impressive: the radar array from a Chelonian sky-maiden! Sky-maidens are the terror of Galaxy 16. Parents tell their children about them. Scary bedtime stories about maidens falling like stars from the heavens, burning the sky in their wake...'

'So, what is this?' asked Amy. 'Is this more of your enemies ganging up on you?'

'No,' the Doctor said with a smile. 'This is an Empire warship. The Empire of Eternal Victory!' He spun on his heels and waved up at Captain Jones. 'Captain! So nice to meet you! How long has it been since this ship first contacted you?'

Captain Jones blinked slowly at the newcomer on her bridge. The muscles in her jaw bulged as she ground her teeth together. Rory thought she was about to lose her temper – but Sam stepped forward just in time.

'These are the travellers who arrived in the unauthorised transport capsule, ma'am,' he said. 'They were responding to our distress signal. This is the Doctor, and his friends are...'

'Captain Viola Jones, Earth Corp Couriers,' the

captain said, staring straight at the Doctor.

'Couriers?' Rory said.

The Doctor nodded. 'The ECC. Intergalactic postmen!'

Captain Jones looked a little miffed – she obviously didn't like to be called a postman. 'Explain yourself,' she said, her voice sounding grave. 'Do you know this ship?'

The Doctor dashed across the control room and up the steps to Captain Jones's station. He grinned at her, then pointed at the screen. 'The warship? No, not exactly. But I've seen ones like it before. I take it that the crew have issued threats and demanded that you hand over whatever technology you have to offer?'

The captain sighed angrily. 'Indeed,' she said. 'We're carrying a cargo of important medical equipment to an Earth colony on Hephestus Beta. The doctors there have only very basic facilities – this equipment is to help them fight off an outbreak of the Orion flu.'

The Doctor breathed in sharply, baring his

teeth. 'Nasty.'

'That's why we need to get to Hephestus Beta quickly,' the captain said, flashing a frustrated glare at the warship on the viewscreen. 'These attackers are causing a considerable delay.'

'Oh, they'll do more than delay you,' said the Doctor. He smiled, but it was cold and without mirth. 'In my experience, when the Empire of Eternal Victory set their sights on you, it's best to run.' He stopped smiling and stared straight at the captain. 'So, why are your engines switched off?'

Captain Jones stared at him, her eyebrows high in an expression of shock. Rory had seen that look before. People were often surprised by the Doctor.

'The engines are not switched off,' she replied. Her voice was sharp, her words like little knives. She obviously wasn't used to being bossed around like this. 'They're not working.'

'Oh, dear,' said the Doctor. 'Why not?'

Captain Jones was still glaring at the Doctor, not entirely sure why she should answer him. Instead, Sam cleared his throat and spoke up. 'We got stuck on something in the asteroid field. We're not sure what. We tried to power up the engines to maximum, to get ourselves free – but it didn't work. Whatever had us stuck just wasn't letting us go.'

'Was it some sort of trap?' asked the Doctor. 'A tractor beam from the Empire ship? Some sort of energy field?'

'No, it can't have been that,' Sam said.

Captain Jones chipped in. 'We were trapped here a few hours before the other ship arrived,' she said. 'The *Black Horizon* seems to be attached to some sort of… cable.'

'A cable?' the Doctor said.

'We're really not sure what it is,' the captain admitted with a sigh. 'Look,' she added, pointing at the bottom corner of the viewscreen.

The Doctor followed Captain Jones's finger, his eyes narrowing. He craned his neck and squinted harder. Rory looked too, but all he could see was a white line in the corner of the screen. It shone in the light from Gloriana XVI and from the

Black Horizon's navigation beacons. It did look something like a cable, but no cable Rory had ever seen before. Its surface was uneven, covered in bumps and blobs, and it glistened wetly in the starlight. It led off into the distance, disappearing between two of the larger asteroids.

'That's no cable,' the Doctor said, his face looking pale.

Captain Jones's brows crinkled, and she opened her mouth to ask a question – but just then, the robotic voice echoed around the spaceship again.

'This is your final warning!' it screeched. 'You will be boarded in five minutes. Prepare to surrender!'

The Doctor whirled round to face Captain Jones. 'Where will they board?'

'Deck six, the main airlock,' she replied, looking a little shaken by the Doctor's urgency. 'That would make the most sense.'

'Excellent!' The Doctor pointed at Amy. 'Pond, you're with me. And guards! We'll need guards.' He jumped down from the platform and moved towards the exit. Amy followed him.

The captain, her eyes wide in surprise, nodded at the small squad of security guards on the bridge. They saluted, then joined Amy and the Doctor at the door.

'Rory,' the Doctor added, 'you stay here with Sam and the good captain.'

'But, but…' Rory was stammering, trying to keep up with the Doctor's lightning-fast pace.

'Oh, come now, Rory. I'm sure we won't be long.' The Doctor smiled. 'We'll just say hello, shake a few robotic hands, have a chat. It'll be sorted in just a few minutes, then we'll be right back.'

The door swished open and the Doctor dashed through it into the brightly lit corridors beyond. Amy smiled at Rory, waved goodbye, then followed him. The guards – as confused as everyone else by the Doctor's whirling style – marched quickly after them.

CHAPTER 3
INVASION

Amy was starting to get a stitch. It was amazing, how much running she had to do. Didn't the Doctor ever have to stop for breath?

The guards were keeping up, though. They were all grim-faced and stoic, very serious indeed. Amy wanted to stop and tickle one of them, just to lighten the mood. But then again, perhaps that wasn't the best idea. They had guns, after all…

They had travelled down in a lift, and run through a number of identical white corridors, turning many corners. Amy knew she'd be lost if she had to find her own way back. The *Black Horizon* was like a maze.

As they turned a final corner, the Doctor stopped dead. Amy stumbled to a halt, her boots thundering on the smooth floor. The guards stopped, too.

At the end of this corridor, there was a large, white door. It was made of thick metal plates, and its handle was a thick, heavy metal bar about a metre long. A sign was set in the wall above the door, which said, "MAIN AIRLOCK: CAUTION!"

But it wasn't the door that had stopped everyone in their tracks. They could all see a point of white-hot light burning in the upper right corner of the airlock door. It hissed and sizzled, slowly moving in a clockwise direction around the edge of the door.

'They're cutting through,' Amy whispered, feeling scared.

The Doctor suddenly leaped forward, the sonic screwdriver buzzing in his hand. Its green light washed over the metal door. 'There we go,' he said. 'I've agitated the molecules in the metal, raising its melting point. We've got a few more minutes before they will be able to cut through. Now...'

He looked all around himself, at the floors, wall and ceiling – then he spotted a small door set in to the corridor's wall. It was no bigger than a kitchen cupboard door. The Doctor popped it open, revealing a little cubby-hole full of all sorts of bric-a-brac. There were tools, and pieces of scrap metal and plastic. There were piles of oily rags and small containers full of screws.

The Doctor swept the whole lot out, letting it clatter to the floor.

He looked down at his messy handiwork and smiled. 'Right, all of you! I need you to find all the junk you can. Anything, absolutely *anything* – tools, machinery, clothes, rubbish, *anything*. Bring it back here and just throw it on the floor.' He looked up at the guards. 'Come along! Quick as you like!' He clapped his hands, grinning madly.

The bewildered guards slowly stumbled off to do as they were told. Amy looked around, too, finding a small room off to one side which contained spacesuits and breathing apparatus.

She hauled a couple of armfuls of stuff into the corridor and threw it down on the floor.

Before long, the guards started to return one by one. They brought with them all sorts of tools, machinery, gadgets and junk. Someone threw down a pile of grubby overalls. Someone else tipped the contents of a waste-paper bin onto the floor. A third guard opened a toolbox and scattered its contents on top of the growing pile of rubbish.

The Doctor grinned. 'This is perfect! Make it look just like a scrapyard!'

Before long, that's exactly what it did look like. The Doctor picked his way through the junk. He waved everyone back, so they all stood a safe distance away from the airlock door.

The cutting beam had now worked its way all the way around the door. There was a few seconds of silence, then the door fell forward, hitting the floor with a clang. Huge plumes of smoke washed out of the new opening. Amy could see lights in the smoke, moving slowly forward. She could hear the wheeze and whir of machinery from the other side of the door.

Silhouettes started to form in the light of the corridor. The invaders were shaped roughly like humans, but with hard angles and sharp corners. They were unmistakably robots.

Their voices, too, were the voices of robots. One loud voice rang out, 'This ship is now the property of the Empire of Eternal Victory. All life forms on-board will immediately...'

Another robot screamed, interrupting the first. 'Sir! Look at that! Is that a coffee machine!?'

Rory nervously stood in the corner of the control room, trying not to get in the way. Captain Jones was sternly issuing orders from her raised platform, and her crew were dutifully carrying them out. They had just received word from the guards accompanying the Doctor and Amy: the enemies had boarded the ship.

The crew never stopped talking to each other, exchanging vital information and news on the ship's condition. Men and women moved from one corner of the bridge to another, stopping to check read-outs or to receive the latest updates. Captain Jones's crew was operating smoothly and efficiently. Rory was sure that, if it were his ship being invaded by unknown aliens, he wouldn't be able to be as cool under pressure.

Rory watched as Sam crossed the room, carrying a printout from one of the ship's computers. He stopped at the foot of the captain's raised platform and held the paper up for her to see.

Rory could just about make out what Sam was saying. 'Our calculations show that the hull will only last for a few more hours.' The words chilled Rory to the bone. He carefully edged closer, eager to hear more.

Captain Jones snapped the printout from Sam's hand. She glared at the sheet of paper, frowning. 'Are you sure?' she asked.

Sam just nodded in silence, his face pale.

Rory cleared his throat, and Sam and the captain both looked in his direction. 'I couldn't help but overhear... I'm sure the Doctor will be able to sort it all out. He's good at this kind of thing. After all, he's already gone off to face these Eternal Victory blokes…'

Captain Jones sighed. 'That's not what we're worried about. It's the cable. It's stuck on to our ship and it just won't let go. The strain on our hull is threatening to pull the ship to pieces. Look…'

The captain pressed a few buttons on the console in front of her, then pointed to the giant viewscreen on the other side of the room. Rory could see the dark shapes of the asteroids slowly turning in space and, at the bottom of the screen, the white line of the 'cable' that had got stuck to the ship.

But just then, Rory thought he saw something else. Something huge and white and shining, glinting in the dim light of the stars. It moved quickly behind the rocky bulk of an asteroid, disappearing out of view.

'What was that?' he gasped.

'What?' said the captain. 'I didn't see anything.'

'There.' Rory pointed at one corner of the

screen. The captain shifted the angle, zooming in on the asteroid Rory was pointing at. 'Something moved. Behind that asteroid, something *moved!*'

Sam checked another computer nearby. 'Captain, there are no other ships in the area. Just the *Black Horizon*, and the enemies' vessel.'

'I swear to you,' Rory said, 'something moved out there. Something big.'

Suddenly, a tremor shook the room. Rory flung his hand out to the wall to steady himself, and he saw the crew do the same, grabbing on to anything to keep themselves upright. The captain barked, 'Appleseed, what was that?'

Sam checked a few readings. 'The cable is shifting, Captain.'

Rory moved to Sam's side and looked at the computer screens. It was all nonsense to him: lines of calculations whirling by, flashing lights of all sorts of colours, a string of messages scrolling endlessly across a small screen. He had no idea what any of it meant. Sam, however, was staring intently at it all, taking it in.

Within a few seconds, Captain Jones had stepped down to join them, staring at the computer screens, too. Her voice was quiet and serious. 'I need a full scan of that thing immediately.'

'Already doing it, Captain,' Sam replied, barely looking up from the screens.

Another tremor rocked the control room.

'Come on, Sam,' she whispered. 'We need to know what it is, now.' Captain Jones seemed suddenly softer, more encouraging – no more the stern commander Rory had met a few minutes ago. She might appear to be tough and no-nonsense, he thought, but she obviously cared deeply about the people who worked for her.

Sam suddenly stood upright, looking down at the screens in shock. 'That's impossible.'

'What is?' Rory said. 'What's happening?'

'The cable is…' Sam shook his head and pressed a few more buttons. He continued to stare at the screen in disbelief. 'The cable is organic,' he said.

'Organic?' said the captain. 'You mean it's *alive*?'

'Not exactly,' Sam replied. 'But it looks like

it's been made by a living creature. The cable is constructed mainly of carbon, and it's coated in some sort of organic adhesive, too. But there's more than that. It is covered with all sorts of traces of metal. Iron, aluminium, titanium – but it's all rusted away to practically nothing.'

The captain swallowed nervously. 'They sound like the kind of metals you find in starship hulls,' she whispered.

Sam's eyebrows bunched up. He looked confused. 'This isn't normal rust,' he said. 'It's not *old* enough…'

'What do you mean?' Rory asked.

Sam glanced at him, his eyes filled with worry. 'Well, rust is old, right? That's kind of the point of rust – metal lies out in the elements, and it rots away and gets rusty,' he said. 'But we can check the age of this rust with our computers. It's less than a few months old, but that metal is tough and shouldn't have rusted that much in so short a time.'

Rory nodded, understanding – just as another thought occurred to him. 'Wait, you said things only rust when they're exposed to the elements, like the wind and rain,' he said. 'But there's no wind and no rain in space. So, what made the metal rust?'

Rory glanced at the main screen again, just as the control room trembled once more. He could see the cable shaking in space – as if something, somewhere, was hitting it.

'So,' he said, his voice trembling as much as the spaceship, 'whatever this cable is... do we think it's trapped other starships before?'

Sam and the captain looked at each other, then nodded.

'They just dissolved away to rust,' Rory guessed, gulping nervously. 'And now we're next.'

'But this doesn't make any sense,' the captain said. She was starting to sound a little panicked. 'Why would a living thing make a strand of organic cable to trap starships in the middle of an asteroid field?'

Another thump, and the control room shook once more.

Rory stared at the viewscreen, squinting at the shadowy spaces between the asteroids, certain he'd seen something moving again. Suddenly, his heart sank. There, in the cold darkness of space, a gigantic white shape rose from behind an asteroid.

Rory gasped in shock, then sighed, 'But that's impossible…'

It was a spider.

An impossible spider!

Rory had never seen anything like it. It was shining white, and the size of a skyscraper. And it was moving towards the ship.

Its carapace glittered like shattered glass. Its long legs curved around the rock, shaking the cable as they touched it. Rory now knew that the *Black Horizon* wasn't caught on a cable. It was caught in a web.

Captain Jones gasped in shock, and Sam just stared at the viewscreen, his jaw slack with amazement. The rest of the crew had fallen silent.

Slowly, ever so slowly, the spider walked forward. Its spindly legs looked as delicate as ice, and its tiny pinpoint feet seemed to brush the strand of web with the gentlest touch. But each of the creature's footsteps sent a jolt through the *Black Horizon*.

Rory watched the crew members on the bridge. They tried to carry on with their duties, but they all wore expressions of shock and worry. As each shudder passed through the ship, they staggered about, grabbing hold of desks and railings for support.

Rory turned back to the viewscreen and took a closer look at the spider. Now, he could see its head. Spiny mandibles quivered in its jaws, brushing each other in a rapid, hungry motion. It was like someone licking their lips before eating a big roast dinner.

And then Rory realised what fate lay in store for the *Black Horizon*.

'You want to know why that thing traps spaceships in its web?' he said to Captain Jones.

'Yes, of course I do,' the captain snapped.

'Well, why do spiders catch things in their webs? I think we're just like a fly.'

'What?' The captain was confused.

'You know what spiders do to flies, don't you?' Rory said. 'They eat them…'

Another tremor shook through the ship. The lights in the control room flickered and died. The room was plunged into darkness – the only light came from the viewscreen and its picture of the giant spider stalking towards the *Black Horizon*…

CHAPTER 4
FALLING

Just as the Doctor had planned, the robots had been distracted by the piles of junk. They were busily sorting through it all, picking up little scraps, turning them in the light to examine them, then throwing them aside.

Amy watched them, fascinated by their different shapes and sizes. They seemed as cobbled-together as their spaceship, like they'd been put together from a pile of old spare parts. Some of them were tall and fearsome, gleaming with cutting-edge technology – but some were small and weedy, whizzing around on worn rubber tires. One robot was thin and spindly – his legs looked like fishing rods. Another only had one arm, and that arm only had two fingers. A third robot was short and stubby and rolled around on a pair of rubber wheels.

But, despite the differences in their shapes, the robots all had one thing in common: each one wore a mask.

Well, Amy couldn't tell if they were masks, or whether they were what passed for the robots' actual faces. Whatever they were, they were the most striking thing about the invaders. The masks seemed to be made of shards of mirrored metal, studded with jewels. They twinkled in the light, almost beautiful – although the masks were set in fierce expressions, clearly meant to frighten their foes.

'What's with their masks?' Amy asked the Doctor, her voice a careful whisper.

The Doctor turned towards Amy – but he didn't tear his gaze away from the robots, clearly wanting to keep an eye on them. 'They're the hallmark of the Empire of Eternal Victory,' he said. 'Precious metals, exquisite jewels… The warriors of the Empire built these masks out of the spoils of their previous conquests.'

'Couldn't they just go to *H. Samuel*, like anyone else?'

The Doctor smiled. 'Look closer, though, Amy – they're more than masks.'

Amy peered closely at the robots' masks as they picked through the junk on the corridor floor. They caught the light from all directions, glinting and glittering with flashes of dazzling colour. The dancing, sparkling light made it hard to see what the Doctor wanted Amy to see – but, as she squinted, she caught it. A movement, ever so slight. Not just a flash of light glancing off a shard of metal; the mask itself had moved, altered.

A robot looked up at Amy and the expression on its jewelled mask *changed*: it shifted into a scowl. This robot was tall and stocky, his heavy body made up of thick, angular sheets of metal. His mask was encrusted with dark red jewels, like rubies. He stood at the front of the group, and he was obviously their leader: bigger, stronger, fiercer than the others.

He stood up to his full height – Amy reckoned he was easily seven feet tall – and took a couple of steps towards her and the Doctor. She watched the squad of guards nervously raise their guns higher.

The ship shook violently once again. The robots seemed to pay it no attention, but Amy staggered unsteadily across the corridor. She grabbed the Doctor's shoulder for support and said, 'What's doing that? Is that the robots?'

The Doctor did not reply. He stood at the head of the group of nervous guards, staring straight ahead at the invaders. His expression was unreadable.

When the Doctor spoke at last, his voice was quiet and measured. 'Take what you wish from what we have offered you.'

The robot with one arm was trying to fix an electric toothbrush to its shoulder, where his other arm should be. He set it off by mistake and it fell buzzing to the floor. The robot emitted a little electronic squeak of surprise.

The leader of the robots kicked aside an old microwave oven then turned his blood-red mask to the Doctor. He frowned in rage. 'This material is worthless,' he said in his grating metallic voice. 'It is junk!'

'It is all we have to give you,' the Doctor said, calmly.

The robot stepped slowly towards the Doctor, his heavy feet clomping on the floor. He stared down at the Time Lord, who was a good foot shorter. 'You are lying,' he rumbled.

'Maybe,' the Doctor replied. 'But it's all you're getting.'

The robot stood up to his full, impressive height. 'I am Commander Designate Gluon-Alpha-Sierra-Zero-1 of the Great and Shining Empire of Eternal Victory,' he boomed, his mask sparkling.

'Do you make your names from rubbish, just like your bodies?' said the Doctor.

There was a tense pause. Zero-1's mask shifted,

deepening his frown. 'Our sensors detected large amounts of advanced technology in the cargo hold of this ship. We will take it.' He turned to his fellow robots. 'Forward!'

As one, the robots dropped the various bits of rubbish they were holding and filed forward.

The Doctor turned to the guards and whispered, 'Let them pass. I don't want anyone getting hurt.'

The other robots followed Zero-1. They paraded past the guards, who all shuffled timidly out of the way, letting them pass.

As the robots reached a junction in the corridor, another quake shook the ship. The other tremors had made Amy wobble, but this one sent her flying – along with all the scattered rubbish in the corridor. The guards were knocked off their feet, too, as were the robots. The Doctor lashed out, desperately trying to find something to hang on to – but he was too late.

Amy felt the world turn sideways, and everything swirled around her. The last thing she saw before the lights went out was the whole corridor turning on its side, catching the robots unawares and sending them tumbling down another passageway. She heard the clatter and clang of metal as they fell.

Amy flung her arms out to find the Doctor, and they both crashed sideways through a doorway. The guards yelled as they were thrown around outside – each of them made a *thump* noise as they hit the walls of the corridor.

The world kept spinning, and Amy felt just like a towel in a tumble drier.

As she fell, whirling through the air, she thought, 'I just hope I land somewhere safe!'

Sam got to his feet and flung forward a huge red lever on a console.

Rory heard a *thrum* as the emergency power cranked into action. Dark red light filled the room, giving the crew just enough illumination to work by. He looked around himself and saw the crew shakily standing up and returning to their posts.

Sam was already reading data from his bank

of computers. 'We lost artificial gravity on some decks, Captain – and it's still not working right in some parts of the ship. I'll try to get it up and running again…'

That last tremor had been a big one. It had thrown everyone to the floor, and sent a few people flying into the hard edges and sharp corners of consoles. A few people were nursing cuts and bruises. He carefully eyed them all up, one by one, but no one appeared to be seriously injured. Within a couple of minutes, the crew had returned to their stations.

Rory staggered to his feet and stared at the viewscreen. The spider was closer than ever now, its dazzling white form filling up the whole screen.

'Amy,' he muttered out loud, 'I hope you're all right.'

He walked over to the captain's post and looked up at her with pleading eyes. 'We need to get to the Doctor,' he said.

'All in good time, Rory,' she replied. She pressed a button on her computer, opening a communication channel across the whole ship. She raised her voice, her words echoing round the room, silencing everyone. 'Crewmen will return to their duties. Anyone currently off duty is to report to the bridge *immediately*.'

She looked down at Rory. She was chewing her lip, obviously thinking hard about what decision to make. 'Okay,' she said at last. 'Ensign Appleseed, I want you to accompany Rory in a search for the Doctor. You must fully appraise the Doctor of the situation with the spider as soon as possible.'

'But ma'am,' Sam stammered, 'I should stay here and try to help –'

Captain Jones raised a hand to interrupt him. 'You,' she said sternly, 'will follow your orders.'

He bowed his head. 'Yes, ma'am.'

Rory smiled. 'Thank you, Captain,' he said.

Sam saluted his captain and turned to join Rory. Together, they jogged quickly out of the control room in search of the Doctor and Amy...

CHAPTER 5
DESCENT

With the main power out, the corridors were dark and cold. Sam led the way in silence. At each junction he would stop and lean around the corners, checking that the way was clear. He would then wave back to Rory as a signal to follow him further into the darkness.

The ship was mostly quiet – but there were still sounds to be heard. There was an occasional creak as another shake of the spiderweb strained the hull.

They reached another junction. Sam pointed off to the left and whispered, 'The Doctor and Amy should be over in that direction, but that's the part of the ship where the gravity is malfunctioning.'

'Is that serious?'

'I hope not. They might have taken a tumble, but I'm sure they'll be okay.' Sam checked the other corridors for signs of life. Then, happy they were still alone, he waved Rory on.

They slowly tiptoed in silence for a few more minutes, passing through more dark and empty corridors. Sam's crewmates were safely gathered on the bridge. The rest of the ship was deserted – or it should have been deserted…

Rory was sure he could hear something from behind him. A faint electric whirring noise, like a little motor.

He grabbed Sam's shoulder and pulled gently, bringing the young soldier to a halt. As quiet as a mouse, he whispered, 'I think we're being followed.'

Sam glanced behind Rory and nodded, pointing. Rory looked too – and saw a dim, blue light bobbing through the gloom towards them.

Sam and Rory quickly dodged round the nearest corner. Rory's heart was racing. He was suddenly breathing so loudly that he hoped that whatever was following them couldn't hear it!

The whirring sound was getting closer and closer...

Rory quickly looked around, and saw a cupboard door hanging loose on the wall. It had obviously been damaged in all the tremors that had been shaking the ship. It was only held on by a single hinge – and that one was badly broken. With a gentle tug, Rory yanked the door from the wall.

He flattened his back against the wall, right by the corner. He gripped the broken door tightly with both hands and held his breath. The whirring was getting closer still...

Just as the sound reached the corner, Rory jumped out with a loud yell!

He swung the door wildly into the corridor and it hit something with a deafening CLANG!

There was an electronic shriek of pain and surprise. Rory had hit a robot – in fact, he'd hit the little thing so hard that he'd knocked one of his arms off!

The little robot spun in circles on tiny rubber

wheels, squealing in terror. He raised his remaining arm to shield his face – a plain mask made of rusted metal, set in an expression of terror.

'Please don't hurt me!' the machine cried. 'Mercy! Mercy! I surrender!'

The Doctor and Amy lay in a heap of mops and brooms. They'd landed in some sort of storeroom. Amy looked up and saw the door. Beyond it, the corridor was filled with the blood-red glow of emergency lighting. A loose panel flapped open from the wall, swinging with the rhythm of the tremors that still shook the ship.

She pulled herself to her feet and saw the Doctor doing the same. He knocked aside a jumble of plastic buckets as he did so, and his foot got caught in the handle of one. He shook his leg until the bucket rattled off into the darkness.

He looked up at the door, too. 'Well, that's not good.'

'Everything's sideways,' said Amy.

'Something moved the ship,' the Doctor said.

The Doctor jumped up and down three times, then swayed slightly on his tiptoes. He nodded to himself. 'Yes, thought so. The artificial gravity is on the fritz. Just in this part of the ship – we're sideways, everything else isn't. This is not good at all.'

'What could do that? Those robots?'

'Come on,' the Doctor said, ignoring her questions. He started to climb a set of shelves, heading towards the door. 'The robots could be anywhere on the ship by now. We've got to find them – and stop them.'

When he reached the door, the Doctor hauled himself up to stand on the wall of the corridor outside. Amy was about to follow him when she noticed something lying in one of the scattered buckets. The Doctor's sonic screwdriver. It must have fallen from his pocket in the confusion.

'Doctor, wait!' she called after him. 'You've –'

'Come along, Pond!' he shouted back. 'There's no time to lose.'

Sighing, she knelt down to pick up the device. She slipped it into her jacket pocket and then clambered up the shelves after him. The climb was awkward: for a start, the shelves were sideways and they were still cluttered with bottles and rags, all sorts of cleaning materials. It was sometimes hard to get a good footing, but Amy finally made it up to the corridor, where she leant on the Doctor's shoulder and took a moment to catch her breath.

'The airlock's that way,' the Doctor said, nodding into the red gloom. He took a few steps towards it, then stopped at a junction in the corridors. What used to be a crossroads was now a chasm. Their corridor stretched off into the darkness ahead of them but, beneath their feet and turned on its side, another corridor had turned into a shaft that plunged into blackness.

Above their heads, another corridor rose away from them. Looking up, Amy could see the scorch marks made by the robots when they had cut into the ship.

'There's the airlock,' she said, pointing up.

'So, the robots must have fallen down there,' the

Doctor added, pointing down. 'Wait a minute…'

The Doctor dashed back to the storeroom, crouched down at the edge of the door, and reached inside. Seconds later, he returned with a rope.

He tied one end of the rope to a metal handrail on the side of the corridor above their heads — the side that was now their ceiling. He dropped the other end down into the darkness. He tugged the rope sharply a couple of times, then grinned.

Amy's heart was sinking. 'We're not going to…'

'We are!' said the Doctor. 'What's the matter? Never been abseiling?'

'Not on a crashed spaceship filled with killer robots in the middle of an asteroid field. No.'

The Doctor laughed. 'There's a first time for everything!' he said. Taking a tight hold of the rope, he took a step backwards towards the shaft. The handrail creaked slightly, and Amy saw the rope straining under the Doctor's weight. But by now, the Doctor's head was already disappearing over the edge.

Amy gulped. She stepped up to the rope, grabbed hold, and started to descend.

On their way down, they passed door after door. Some were closed, but through the open ones Amy could see the sideways remains of all sorts of rooms: mess halls, dining areas, kitchens, laboratories, bedrooms. Everything in the rooms had tumbled messily as the ship had turned on to its side. Tables had flipped over. Chairs had tumbled everywhere. Glass cups and beakers had shattered on impact, the fragments glinting like rubies in the red emergency light.

'This is confusing,' Amy said as she lowered herself slowly down. 'How much of the ship is on its side?'

'Oh, not all that much,' the Doctor called up to her. 'I can just about feel the edge of the normal artificial gravity field below us. Less chit-chat, Pond. More climbing.'

Their descent was tough work – made tougher by the constant tremors that still shook the ship, sending the rope swaying this way and that. Amy's arms were tired. The Doctor, on the other hand, seemed to be enjoying himself.

'I think I can see the floor,' he said. 'Well, the wall. Well, you know what I mean.'

'How much further?'

'Just a few more metres.'

Amy wondered if she could just jump down now. Would the fall hurt that much? Could it be any worse than the pain in her exhausted arms?

They descended a little further, passing another open door. This room was dark. The emergency lighting didn't seem to be working properly and Amy couldn't see anything inside. Except for…

Something glinted in the red light from outside. Something moving…

'Doctor!' she yelled. 'Look out!'

One of the robots burst out of the doorway. This one had a squat head and a mask made of jet-black crystal. His body looked rusty and old – but he still moved quickly, like lightning.

And instead of an arm, he had a vicious-looking

circular saw. With a screech and a whine, the saw started spinning. Its shiny, sharp teeth turned to a blur as it spun faster and faster.

Amy kicked against the wall, swinging herself and the Doctor away from the door.

'Woah!' the Doctor cried beneath her, as he desperately tried to keep hold of the rope. 'Be careful!'

Now the rope was swinging back towards the robot. He jabbed his saw arm into the air towards them, but he was still too far away.

She kicked the wall again, sending them swinging in the opposite direction. 'What do you *think* I'm doing?'

As they reached one wall of the shaft, the Doctor flung his arm out and grabbed a handrail. He locked his elbow around it, stopping them in mid-swing. He pulled hard, straining to keep them at a safe distance from the robot. 'We can't stay here for ever!' he gasped. 'If we're going to keep climbing down, I'm going to have to let go.'

'Wait a second, wait a second,' said Amy. 'When

I say "now", let go.'

'I do hope you know what you're doing.'

The robot reached further out, sweeping his saw back and forth into the corridor. 'We shall take your technology!' he squawked.

'Now!' Amy cried, kicking against the wall. The Doctor let go of the handrail, and the rope started to swing swiftly back towards the door. The robot was balancing itself on the very edge of the doorframe, raising his saw menacingly. Amy clenched her jaw. 'Take *this*, pal!'

She kicked out her leg as they swung back past the door. Her boot hit the robot's face hard, cracking his black mask. He screeched as he tumbled back into the room.

'Down, Doctor!' Amy yelled. 'Head down *now*!'

They scrambled down the rope as fast as they could. Amy heard clattering and scraping and more electronic yelps from above as they slid down, getting ever closer to solid ground. *Not far now,* she thought. *Not far…*

But still too far!

The robot, screaming with electronic rage, burst from the doorway again. Amy ducked, feeling the whoosh of the saw blade pass over her head. The shock of the attack made her loosen her grip for a moment, and she slid too fast down the rope. She heard the Doctor say, 'Ow!' as her boots hit his head.

Still screeching, the robot lashed out again – and this time, he hit. Amy watched in horror as the blade ripped into the rope, the strands of material fraying away to nothing.

With a *snap*, the rope tore in two.

Amy's stomach lurched, as she and the Doctor fell...

CHAPTER 6
HISTORY

Rory had never seen a machine quake in fear before. He never knew it was even possible. But the little robot in front of him shook and shivered, all the parts of his metal body clanking noisily. The panels on its rusted face mask trembled in an expression of meek terror.

Rory dropped the cupboard door that he was still holding. 'It's all right,' he said, raising his open hands. 'We're not going to hurt you.'

'N-n-not going to hurt me?' the robot stammered. His voice was high-pitched and nervous. 'You knocked my arm off!'

Rory scooped the arm off the floor. 'I'm sorry!

I'm sorry! Is there any way to fix it?'

'Fix it?' Sam hissed. 'We should just shoot the thing! He's one of the robots from the Empire of Eternal Victory!'

'I know,' sighed Rory, 'but look at him! He's hardly a threat.'

The robot continued to tremble nervously. His eyes swung first to Rory, then to Sam – back and forth, pleadingly.

Rory asked him, 'Do robots have names?'

'We do,' the robot said, his eyes darting to stare at Rory.

'So, what's yours?'

'I am Retrieval Bot Designate Meson-Zero-Sierra 29,' he said. 'But the other robots call me Messy.' His mask drooped sadly with a soft creaking noise.

Looking at the ramshackle machine, Rory could see how he got his nickname. No one part of Messy matched another. One arm was long and thin (that was the one Rory had knocked off), the other was short and stumpy. His body was lumpy and uneven; the metal casing was covered in dents and scrapes and flaky, old paint. Instead of legs, Messy had wheels. Well, he had one wheel on one side – on his other side, he was fitted with a threadbare rubber caterpillar track.

Rory knelt next to Messy and lifted the broken arm to its socket, trying to find how to reattach it. There were loose wires and bent pins, but he couldn't see what was meant to fix to what. 'I'm sorry, Messy,' he said at last, 'I just can't work out how to do this.'

Messy sighed, his rickety body tinkling as it slumped in misery. 'That's all right,' he said. 'Nothing ever works properly, anyway. I always get the worst scraps and the broken parts.'

Rory looked up at Sam, who was pacing impatiently around the junction. 'And these are the terrifying invaders you were worried about?'

'Oh, but we *are* terrifying!' Messy said, his voice sounding more hopeful than certain. 'We are the shining, glorious, amazing and really, really scary Empire of Eternal Victory!'

Sam raised an eyebrow and smirked. 'Really, really scary?' he said.

Messy nodded. 'Oh, yes,' he said with pride. 'Really scary.'

Rory and Sam glanced at each other and burst out laughing. They just couldn't help themselves.

'You're not scary,' said Rory. 'I'm really sorry to say it, but you're not. I mean, I attacked you with a cupboard door and you screamed in terror!'

Messy jigged about uncertainly on his wheels. 'You took me by surprise,' he said. 'I wasn't expecting anyone to swing a cupboard door at me.'

'I broke your arm off!'

'It was meant to do that!' Messy yelped, pulling himself up to his full height. (At his full height, he reached about as high as Rory's waist – so this wasn't a terribly impressive sight.)

Rory and Sam started laughing again, and Messy shrank sadly into the corner. 'This always happens,' he moaned.

Pulling himself together, Rory smiled warmly down at the little robot. 'Oh, come on, don't be sad. It's all right, I know someone who can fix you up in no time. You'll be as good as new!'

Messy's eyes curved up at Rory. 'Like I was back in the Plumbing Department?'

'If that's where you were made' Rory replied, 'then yes – just like back then.'

Messy sprang back into life again, whizzing round Rory in an excited circle. 'I never wanted to fight,' he chirped. 'I was happy back in Plumbing.'

Rory whirled around too, trying to keep up with Messy. He was starting to feel dizzy, so he stepped away from the robot so he could stand still again. 'You were a plumber?'

'Oh, yes,' Messy said. 'Back when the first Empire of Eternal Victory was still in power. They built all sorts of robots to do their work. I worked for the Emperor's office – lots of very important pipes to clean and sinks to unblock! But the Empire also built whole armies of other robots to wage their wars for them.'

'What happened to the first Empire?' Rory asked.

'They disappeared,' Messy said. He stopped spinning and appeared to think for a moment. 'Or they died out. Or they were defeated. No one remembers what happened. One day they were the rulers of half the galaxy, then the next… they were gone.'

'No one remembers?' said Rory.

'Well,' said Messy, 'I'm sure we robots would have been able to remember it all – we were there, after all. But we purged our historical databanks after the first Synthetic Emperor took the throne. He decreed that the first Empire was weak and foolish, and demanded that all records of them were destroyed. All the true stories of the first Empire were deleted. Every robot was forced to have their personal memory banks wiped, too.'

'So, you were there, but…?'

'I don't remember a thing about it,' Messy admitted.

'How long ago did all this happen?'

'Oh, just one or two thousand years ago,' said Messy.

Rory blinked in surprise. 'And you were alive when the first Empire was still in power? How old does that make you?'

'Like I said – one or two thousand years old.'

'Crikey,' said Rory, 'no wonder you look so battered.'

'It's not just age that makes me look like this, though,' Messy said, sadly. 'You should see our finest warriors – they are gleaming and perfect, with the very best weapons and technology.'

'So, why do they get the best gear, and you get to look like that?'

Messy swirled around in a circle, then stopped, staring straight at Rory. 'When the first Empire died out, the robots rose up and took over,' he explained. 'We became the new Empire of Eternal Victory. We set out across the cosmos, defeating our foes, and taking their technology for our own.'

'You steal the technology of other races?' Rory asked.

'Basically, yes,' said Messy. 'The thing is, only the very best warriors get the very best gear. And, like I said… I'm a plumber.' His eyes drooped sadly.

'So,' Rory asked, 'you're here to take the technology aboard this ship?'

Messy nodded again, his eyes jerking up and down.

'I see.'

'But I have been defeated,' Messy said quietly. 'I must surrender myself to my vanquisher as a prisoner of war.'

'Me?' said Rory. 'Your vanquisher? And anyway, I don't want any prisoners! I have to find Amy, and the Doctor.'

'Then I shall help you,' Messy said at last. 'You have defeated me, after all, so I must offer my service to you. It is the way of the Empire.'

Rory sighed. 'Oh, all right then. Come on – we need to hurry up!'

CHAPTER 7
WATERPROOF

Rory and Sam walked on in silence for a few more minutes. Messy rolled behind them, also without saying a word. Rory wasn't too sure about dragging the little robot along with them, but he was stuck with him now and he was going to have to make the best of it. He was sure the Doctor would know what to do with Messy — if they ever found him.

Bathed in the red beams of the emergency lighting, the corridors of the *Black Horizon* were eerie places. Every now and again, Rory would catch sight of something moving at the corner of his eye — but when he turned to look, he just saw his own shadow, stretching off into the dark corners. The air was ice cold, too. Sam had explained that the heating systems were probably on the blink.

There were no sounds apart from the clomp of their own footsteps and the whirr of Messy's engines. Rory was beginning to wonder if they were going the right way. Wherever the Doctor was, Rory could be sure he'd be in the middle of a heap of trouble. And trouble was usually noisy – very noisy!

Just then, Rory thought he heard something. A quiet, tinkling noise, off in the distance. Babbling, splishing, splashing…

He raised a hand, stopping Sam and Messy in their tracks. 'Is that… Is that water?' he whispered.

Sam cocked his head, turning his ear towards the sound. 'I think it is,' he said. He looked around until he found a small glass panel set into a nearby wall. He touched it and it lit up. Lines and shapes in all sorts of colours slid over its surface, and Sam's fingertips nimbly picked through them all with deft motions until he seemed to find what he wanted.

'What's that?' Rory asked.

'It's a data panel,' Sam said. 'It shows all sorts of information about the *Black Horizon*. And look here,' he added, pointing at the map of criss-crossed corridors displayed on the screen. 'We're right next to the ship's hydro-sifting plant.'

'We're next to the what?' Rory had never heard of such a thing.

Messy whizzed round in front of Rory and turned his head up to look at him. He had a hopeful expression on his mask. 'If I could be so bold?' he said, timidly. 'Many starships are fitted with a hydro-sifting plant. On lengthy interstellar journeys, organic life forms need a large amount of water to survive – much more than could actually be carried on the ship. The hydro-sifter's main job is to collect waste water and recycle it for use in those times when the ship cannot get a supply of fresh water.'

Rory nodded slowly, understanding. 'Like one of those barrels in your back garden, to collect rain water,' he said. He listened to the noise of the water ahead of them. There were gurgles and drips, splashes and rushes. 'And that sounds like a lot of water,' Rory added.

Sam was looking worried now. He turned back to the data panel and swiped his fingers this way and that across its surface. 'Look at this,' he said. 'Something must have happened in that big jolt before. The whole hydro-sifting plant has gone offline.' He glanced up at Rory, fear in his eyes. 'It's shut down, and its overflowed into the corridors ahead. They're full of water.'

Rory stared into the darkness, listening to the sploshing sounds. 'We've got to get past it. Is there any way around?'

Sam checked the map again. 'The gravity is down in the sectors to either side,' he announced. 'If we want to get past, we're going to have to risk the water.'

'And the airlock is definitely in that direction?' Rory asked. 'The Doctor and Amy are on the other side of the water?'

Sam nodded. 'Yeah,' he said, 'and there's

no other way around it. I hope you're good at swimming.'

Rory nodded. He knew he'd be fine – but then he looked down at his feet and saw Messy. The last time he checked, he didn't think robots could float, let alone swim. 'What about you?' he asked the robot. 'How are we going to get you through?'

'I am a plumbing-bot,' Messy reminded them, a note of pride in his voice. 'I am completely waterproof, and fitted with a small outboard motor in cases of emergency. Blocked drains, burst pipes, floods – none of them hold any fear for me!'

'I wish I had an outboard motor,' Rory sighed. 'You'll probably get across faster than either of us. Come on, then.' Rory started to march into the darkness, towards the sound of rushing water. Sam and Messy followed behind without question or complaint.

Rory thought he probably looked much braver than he felt.

The corridor they were walking along sloped

gradually downwards. Sam had explained that the ramp led down to the level below, before rising again a few dozen metres later. All they had to do was get past this dip, which – as they could all now see – was full of water. On the other side, though, things should be dry and the rest of their journey to the airlock should be simple.

Rory stood at the very edge of this brand new, indoor lake. He looked down to see the water lapping at his trainers. He could feel it soaking through the fabric of his shoes, and it felt icy cold. He shivered as he looked across the surface of the water, imagining the freezing plunge they had ahead of them.

There was very little light here, too – just the blue illumination of the data panels set in the walls. The shimmering surface of the water scattered the light across the ceiling of the corridor. The pattern it made looked like a trembling silver web – and it reminded Rory why they were here, and why they had to get to the Doctor as soon as they could. He took a deep breath to steady his nerves, then he turned to Sam and Messy.

'So, Messy,' Rory said. The little robot buzzed around his feet, splashing up a little of the water on to his jeans. He considered complaining, but then he remembered he was about to get a good deal wetter. He leant down and stared Messy straight in the eye, seeing the tiny electronic cameras hidden behind the mask. 'Are you sure you're going to be okay getting across here? Sam says there should only be about twenty metres of deep water before we'll hit the slope on the other side.'

'My motor is powerful enough to propel me for over five hundred metres before needing a recharge,' Messy explained, as if he was quoting from some sort of "Buy A Robot!" website. 'Please, sir,' he added, 'don't worry about me.'

Sam came to Rory's side. 'We should get moving,' he said. 'We need to take this slowly. We don't know what might be hiding in the water, so we'll have to be careful. And we can't waste any more time if we're going to find the Doctor any time soon.'

Rory nodded in agreement. 'Who's going first?' he asked.

But Messy answered that question for him. The robot whizzed down the last bit of the slope, sloshing into the water without a second thought. Rory heard his outboard motor roar into life and he watched, amazed, as Messy tore through the water, leaving foamy waves in his wake.

Rory laughed, as Messy faded into the darkness. After just a couple of seconds, there was an electronic cry from the shadows, 'I have made it across! I shall wait here for you.'

He turned to Sam, raising an eyebrow. 'So, that's the time to beat,' he said, gesturing towards the cold water. 'Well, after you…'

With a smile, Sam started to wade in, soon finding himself up to his neck. As he pushed himself off the floor and started to swim away, Rory followed him. The water was colder than he'd feared. His breath was snatched from his lungs, and it felt like a fist made of ice was crushing his chest. Rory remembered all those times on holiday when his mum and dad had said he'd 'get used to it' as he stepped off the warm sands of some sunny beach and into freezing seawater. He guessed they were right, though – he always did get used to it. So now, he dove into the water, splashing into the unknown.

It was dark, but Rory could just spot the faint glow of light from the rising passage on the far side of the water, so it was pretty easy to point himself in the right direction. He could hear the steady, rhythmic sound of Sam swimming a few metres ahead of him. All they needed to do was keep swimming, and they'd reach the other side in a minute or two. Simple enough…

Except Rory suddenly became aware that he and Sam weren't the only things swimming through the water. He felt something cold and hard brush against his leg. He stopped swimming and looked down into the inky water, but it was much too dark to see anything down there.

He swam on for a few more seconds, trying to convince himself that he'd imagined it – but there it was again, something sweeping through the water underneath him. He stopped swimming again and then, treading water to keep himself afloat, he peered down into the depths.

Rory's teeth were chattering – but he had no idea if they were reacting to the ice-cold water or the terror.

Sensing that Rory had stopped, Sam paused too, asking, 'What's the matter?'

'There's something down there,' Rory whispered.

'Are you sure?'

'Positive.'

Suddenly, Sam cried off into the distance, 'Messy! Are you still at the other side of the water?'

'Yes, sir,' the robot trilled in response. 'Still waiting here for you.'

'Okay,' said Sam quietly, turning back to Rory. 'I'm not sure that's good news. If there is something down there, it's not our new robot friend.'

'*If* there's something down there?!' Rory hissed. 'There's *definitely* something down there. I can feel it again – there!' Rory splashed around, trying to point at whatever was down there. He had managed to move quick enough, and now they both could see it – a dark shadow beneath the surface, gliding swiftly through the water.

'What is it?' asked Sam.

'I have no idea,' Rory said. He felt ashamed that his voice was getting high pitched – but he was terrified, after all. 'We need to keep moving.'

'It might just be another plumbing robot,' Sam said. 'They seem quite friendly.'

'I'm not hanging around to find out,' said Rory. '*Keep moving!*'

And with that, they both swam for their lives. Every few seconds, they could see the shadow darting through the water. First it swept past their left-hand side, then to the right, then Rory could see it creeping darkly right underneath them.

He thrashed through the water as fast as he could, but the shadow was getting closer, growing in size as it got closer to the surface. Now Rory could see the glint of steel on its body.

It corkscrewed in the water, turning to lie on its back as it closed the gap with Rory. He could see its face now – a jewelled mask, studded with emeralds, set in a sinister grin.

'It's a robot,' cried Rory, splashing forward as fast as his tired, cold arms and legs would carry him. 'Yep, it's definitely a robot. A big one, and it *doesn't* look friendly!'

Ahead of him, Sam finally reached shallow water. He turned and reached out for Rory's hand, grabbing it and heaving him quickly out of the depths.

Messy buzzed around his new friends, agitated, as Rory and Sam stumbled their way out of the shallow water and on to dry land.

Rory was out of breath and freezing cold. His limbs were weak and shaking with exhaustion. But he had no time to rest. Behind them, with a crash of foamy spray, the robot erupted from the water. With an electronic roar, it splashed its way out of the water, making a beeline straight for them.

'Run,' Rory croaked, his voice hoarse. Messy

and Sam got the message, and the three of them tore down the corridor away from the water.

Now it was on dry land, the robot was even faster. It placed one heavy, metal foot in front of the other, marching swiftly after its prey…

CHAPTER 8
CORNERED

Amy was confused. This wasn't what falling should feel like. She and the Doctor had fallen free for only a few seconds before she started to slow down.

It now felt almost like something was pushing them back up. Or at least, trying to.

The Doctor was laughing. As they drifted ever more gently downwards, he waved at Amy, grinning. 'This is fun, isn't it?'

'What's happening?' she said, watching the corridor walls slide slowly past them.

'The ship's artificial gravity is very confused,' he replied. 'One corridor is up, the next one is down – left and right aren't left and right any more. Walls and floors and ceilings… none of it means anything! Who knows where we'll land!'

Amy looked down. Beneath her feet, just a dozen or so metres down, she could see another crossroads in the corridors. Everything was still sideways. So, the passage they were falling down carried on downwards into the darkness. The two other corridors at the junction led off from either side, providing ledges.

Although they were now falling very slowly indeed, Amy could see that they would be at the junction in just a few seconds.

'Doctor,' she said, 'could we grab hold of one of the ledges there? Could we use that to stop ourselves falling?'

He nodded. 'That seems like a very good idea…' A quizzical look crossed over his face. 'Oh. Oh, now that's strange. Very strange indeed.'

Whatever the Doctor was feeling, Amy could feel it as well. Her body wanted to fall downwards, but it was being pushed upwards too. That was strange enough. But now it was starting to feel as if she was being pulled to one side. All these strange forces on her body made it feel like she was being sucked into a plughole, swirling around and around and around.

As the sideways tugging got stronger, Amy flung out a hand, pushing against the side of the corridor. The Doctor did the same – and then he started laughing again. 'Oh, this is perfect!'

'What…' But Amy didn't finish her question.

With a bump and a tumble, the forces on Amy's body suddenly snapped into normality. She fell on to the floor. It was *proper* falling this time – and she had landed on the *proper* floor, right at the centre of the crossroads.

She blinked and looked around herself, confused. 'Would you mind telling me exactly what just happened?' she asked the Doctor.

He smiled. 'The gravity here is back to normal. So it just scooped us up and plonked us back on the floor, where we should be. Perfect!' The Doctor brushed the creases out of his jacket sleeves, making sure he was neat and tidy and ready to face whatever this weird spaceship threw at them next.

'Doctor.'

'Just a moment, Amy, I need to work out where we are.' The Doctor walked to a small glass panel set into the wall. He touched it with his fingertip and it burst into life, showing a three-dimensional map of the ship. There was a pulsing red arrow telling them that "YOU ARE HERE". 'I see, I see,' he muttered to himself. 'We're about halfway between the cargo hold and the command centre. So, if I'm reading this correctly, all we need to do is head down there, take a left, then the second right…'

'Doctor, I really think you should see this.'

The Doctor didn't even look up from the screen. He simply stopped muttering directions to himself and snapped, 'Not now, Amy!'

'Yes, now,' she snapped back at him. 'We've got company.'

A small group of robots – about five or six, Amy guessed – was marching up the corridor towards them. No one robot looked like another but they all had one thing in common. They were all holding guns.

The Doctor took one look and swallowed nervously. 'Come along, time to go!' he said, making towards one of the corridors.

Amy grabbed the collar of his jacket and yanked him back. 'Not that way,' she said. 'That's where we just fell down – that corridor won't work! Come on, this way.'

Amy and the Doctor ran down the corridor as fast their feet would carry them. Through puffs and pants, the Doctor managed to say, 'I'm not sure this is the way we want to go! I need to get to the *Black Horizon*'s cargo hold – but that's in the other direction!'

'We can't go back!'

'We've got to,' the Doctor said, a note of desperation in his voice. 'We have to stop the robots getting their hands on all that medical equipment.'

They could hear the robots marching quickly behind them. Their metal feet were stomp-stomp-

stomping faster and faster, bringing them ever closer.

'We're running out of time,' Amy said. 'We've got to keep moving.'

But where were they moving to? Amy and the Doctor were both fast runners, but she had got a slight head start on him. If this was a race, she'd be in the lead. So, because she was in front, it was down to her to choose which way to go.

They were coming up to another junction. Amy grabbed the Doctor's arm and darted left, dragging him with her. Amy made the choice without any thought. She wasn't really looking either, so she didn't see the small group of people coming the other way. She barely had time to register that she was about to collide with someone before she realised that it was her husband!

Rory grabbed her shoulders and grinned. 'Amy! You're okay!'

She gave a quizzical look to him and Sam, at their soaking wet clothes and the sodden hair plastered to their foreheads. 'What on earth happened to you?'

'I'll explain later.'

Amy looked behind him to see the little robot trundling across the floor. 'I see you've made a new friend.'

'Yeah, and he's not the only one,' Rory said. 'We need to get moving – *now*.'

From the shadows behind Rory, the corridors echoed to a terrible electronic howl.

'Come along, you two,' the Doctor said, whirling around in a circle. 'This way!'

He dashed towards an open door. The others followed him and they quickly found themselves inside a dark room. The Doctor slammed the control panel on the wall and the door slid shut with a hiss. 'They won't find us here,' the Doctor whispered breathlessly.

A red light above the door flicked on, spilling soft light into the room. Amy realised that they were hiding inside the sickbay. A line of empty, neatly-made beds marched away into the darkness. The room went a long way back, hidden behind screens.

The Doctor poked at a few buttons on the door's control panel. A row of little lights on the panel flickered from green to red, and Amy heard a heavy metallic click. 'There,' he said. 'Locked up tight. That should keep us safe for a while. Long enough to work out what to do next…'

In the shadows at the back of the sickbay, Commander Zero-1 stood still and silent. He could be more still and more silent than any organic being – and that's why the humans hadn't noticed him. He'd only come into this room in search of useful technology to scavenge, but he couldn't have guessed at the prize that was in store.

Staying impossibly still and silent, he stood in the gloom and carefully listened to the humans' plan…

CHAPTER 9
RICHES

Zero-1 hadn't seen many humans in his travels. The Eternal Empire had spent centuries conquering galaxy after galaxy – but none of those galaxies had contained many of these strange creatures. It was only as the Empire forged a new path into this galaxy – he believed they called it the Milky Way – that Zero-1 had started to come across the species more and more often.

Humans were fleshy and weak, but that wasn't unusual. Most of the Empire's enemies had been fleshy and weak. They chattered and panicked and dashed around like frightened mice. This latest bunch of humans were brave, though. Zero-1 would grant them that. They had stood up to him and his troops. They seemed to be led by this one called the Doctor: he was a strange human, there was something different about him. Under his leadership, the humans had dared to meet them as they boarded this ship and had demanded that they turn around and leave.

They were funny, Zero-1 decided. This bravery was amusing. But not amusing enough to spare their pitiful lives...

The Doctor was talking now. He was trying to come up with some sort of plan, some way of saving their ship from its inevitable fate. The Doctor could scheme and struggle all he liked, the Empire would still triumph.

From his hiding place at the back of the sickbay, Zero-1 continued to listen in to their conversion. And he soon heard something that would change his plans...

'It was a spider!' the one called Rory said, terror in his voice. (For some reason, Rory and another of the humans had been soaking wet when they arrived in the room. They had quickly found some towels in one of the medical storage cupboards and were doing their best to get dry.)

The girl known as Amy looked sceptical. 'You what? A spider? In space?'

The Doctor nodded, a solemn look on his face. 'A diamondweb spider, one of the rarest creatures in the universe. I knew what it was the minute I saw its web.' He rubbed his chin with his fingers, lost in thought. 'I haven't seen one in centuries,' he whispered to himself. 'I thought they'd all died out. This could be the last of its kind…'

'And we're caught in its web!' The girl was unmoved by the Doctor's reverie.

'That's right,' said the Doctor, 'we are. It's going to eat the *Black Horizon* for breakfast! That's what these spiders do. They feed on metal. They spin their webs in asteroid fields, and catch any stray metal that floats by. Usually, they make do with the ore in floating rocks or all the little bits of glittery spacedust passing through on the solar breeze. Sometimes, their webs even catch comets!'

'Comets?' Rory said with a gasp. 'But they're *huge*!'

'Yes, well, so are diamondweb spiders. And their webs are tough, I mean *really* tough. Strong enough to stop a comet in its tracks, and certainly strong enough to snare the occasional unlucky spaceship.'

'So, that's what the *Black Horizon* is?' Amy said. 'Unlucky?'

'Yes,' said the Doctor. 'The spider doesn't mean us any harm – it's just a big, dumb arachnid, looking for its next meal. Unfortunately, we're it!'

Amy was desperate to find a solution. 'Well, can't we just power up the engines, all the way up to full blast. Wouldn't that be enough to tear us away from the web?'

The Doctor shook his head, and another human – the young male called Sam – spoke up. 'I tried that. I ran the engines at maximum for as long as I could, but the ship couldn't take it. The power shut down, and we didn't move an inch.'

'Well, no, of course you wouldn't have done,'

the Doctor said. 'Once you're stuck to one of these webs, that's pretty much it. Game over! The organic glue created by the spiders is tougher than concrete, and the webs themselves are made from one of the toughest materials in creation. Their webs are made of diamond.'

'The spiders *make* diamond?' Rory sounded hesitant, as if he couldn't quite believe what he had heard.

The Doctor nodded. 'Clever creatures. That's why they're so rare, because who wouldn't want a diamond-making spider as a pet?' He looked sad. 'Rich, bored, *stupid* people all across the galaxy wanted a diamondweb of their own – the perfect fashion accessory, or a factory for the finest jewellery. These billionaires kept them in huge gilded cages, spinning in space, in orbit around their worlds. The whole beautiful species was trapped and caged, one by one, until each spider died, isolated from its kind.'

The Doctor's jaw tightened in determination. 'And that's why we're not going to let anything happen to this one. Even if the Black Horizon itself is destroyed, no one is going to harm that spider. I will find another way to get the crew and their cargo to safety – we've got the TARDIS after all.'

When Zero-1 heard that word, everything changed. He couldn't quite believe it. That ancient word, so full of mystery and power... TARDIS.

This Doctor was no mere human, he was a Time Lord! One of that famous mythical race, designers and creators of so many pieces of delicious technology. If the Doctor had a TARDIS with him, that would be the greatest prize the Empire of Eternal Victory could ever hope to win.

Dominion over all of time, over history itself, was within Zero-1's grasp. And not only that, but there was another prize to be won here: the spider, a potentially infinite source of diamond.

Zero-1's imagination ran wild. He dreamt of a new fleet of ships tearing through creation in the name of the Empire. Sleek craft with shining diamond hulls, practically impervious to damage.

And with the secrets within the TARDIS, those unstoppable ships would be able to travel through time itself in pursuit of conquest and Eternal Victory.

There wasn't a moment to lose. Zero-1 had to strike now!

He marched forward out of the shadows, exulting in the shock and terror the revelation of his presence brought. The humans all took a step away from his imposing metal form.

'Thank you, Doctor,' he said. 'This information is of great value to the Empire.' He pressed a button on his wrist to open a communication channel with his troops. 'I need an update immediately,' he barked.

A tinny voice rang out on Zero-1's communicator. 'We have acquired the human medical equipment. Our troops are returning it to the warship's cargo hold now.'

'Excellent.' Zero-1's mask curled into a sinister smile. 'When that is done, we have a new target. Find the Doctor's time machine. Find the TARDIS and take it to our ship. Once it is safely in our grasp, I want that spider. For the Empire!'

'You can't do this,' the Doctor said. 'I won't let you.'

'You don't have any choice,' Zero-1 said. He lashed out with one robotic claw, grabbing the Doctor's arm tightly. The Time Lord gasped in pain and writhed in his grasp. 'My robots have their orders. They will carry them out, and soon your TARDIS will be mine. But I am not a fool, Doctor, and I know a little about Time Lord technology. I know that I *need* you to help me make your machine work. And I know that your brain is full of plans and blueprints and instructions.' He lifted a metal claw, spreading his fingers over the Doctor's scalp. 'All sorts of delicious Time Lord secrets. I will have those secrets.'

CHAPTER 10
COCOON

In the silence of space, the spider stalked ever closer to the humans' spaceship.

One by one, its long, white legs lifted from the delicate strand of web. They folded and unfolded slowly, curling through space, propelling the spider towards its prey.

Its snow-white carapace glittered in the faint glow of Gloriana XVI. Tiny bumps and ridges caught the light and if you could look close enough, you would see the many tiny crystals embedded in its thick skin. These little jewels shone with all the colours of the rainbow, making the spider shimmer in the black depths of the asteroid field.

The ends of the spider's legs waltzed along the web with ballerina precision. In its zero-gravity home, the creature moved with an impossible poise and elegance. It was hard to believe it was as large as it was. As it finally reached the hull of the *Black Horizon*, though, the spider's size became starkly obvious.

The spaceship bobbed from left to right and up and down, tethered on the thick strand of the spider's web. Almost gently, the spider extended its two front legs and took the spaceship in its grasp. It pulled the ship closer to its body, curling its abdomen towards its target. As they moved, the spider's spinnerets sparkled in the pale starlight. These tiny organs at the end of its abdomen were used to create its unique web – they were the very thing that made the creature so precious, and so rare.

The spinnerets started to tremble and, using its two rear legs, the spider began to pull a thin, white fibre from the organs. This fibre gleamed and glistened as the spider stretched it out towards the ship. The spider carefully placed the fibre against the ship's hull, where it stayed, stuck by a natural glue. Then, it pulled more of the web from the spinnerets, weaving it around and around as it slowly turned the ship.

Within a couple of minutes, the new, fibrous web was turning the ship white. The spider spun the *Black Horizon* endlessly, gluing strand after strand of web to its hull.

The spider had caught its prey, and now it was wrapping it up in a cocoon.

And later, it would return to eat its catch…

The Doctor struggled against Zero-1's steel clutches, but the robot just tightened his grip. He scowled up at his captor.

Just then, a deep, loud creaking noise shook through the room. It sounded like the growl of a giant beast. Sam's face went white. 'The hull… something's happening to the hull,' he said.

The ship lurched, just for a second, and everyone stumbled sideways before managing to steady themselves. 'Oh,' said the Doctor. There was a slight wobble in his voice. 'Now, *there's* an interesting development.'

His communicator crackled into life, and the human captain's voice rang out. 'This is a vital message to all ship's crew. The…' She trailed off momentarily, sounding a little uncertain. 'The spider has reached the *Black Horizon* and is cocooning our ship in its web. All crew members are to make their way to the escape pods and prepare for evacuation on my order.'

'The spider is wrapping the ship up,' said the Doctor. 'Spinning it round, covering it in cobwebs, so it'll be ready to… erm. Well. Eat. Make sure you're prepared, everyone – you may feel the occasional tremor, but the ship's artificial gravity should compensate for most of the motion.'

Zero-1 looked down at the Doctor. 'This ship will be destroyed by the spider, correct?'

The Doctor nodded, a worried look on his face.

'Well, I have an offer to make,' Zero-1 said. 'If you want your friends here to survive, then surrender to me. If not, I will lock them in this room, where they will perish with the ship – and I will take you back anyway, and have your secrets for myself.'

'So, I can't win either way?' the Doctor said. Then, with a sigh, he gave up the fight. 'Fine. Fine, you win. But these people are coming with us. Wherever I go, they go too.'

'Very well.' Zero-1 activated his own communicator and then issued orders to his own crew. 'Find the TARDIS and take it back to our ship. Then prepare the prison cells. We have some visitors…'

CHAPTER 11
PRISONERS

The robots of the Empire of Eternal Victory were stumped.

First of all, they had walked past the time machine several times before they had even realised what it was! They scoured the galaxies for the very finest examples of high technology. A mythical TARDIS was one of the most advanced treasures they could ever hope to find. But not one of them expected it to look like a big, blue, wooden box!

Their computers revealed the truth, though. They waved their little hand-held sensor devices at the blue box, and their colourful screens flickered with messages of confirmation. This was a TARDIS.

So, now they'd identified the thing, all they had to do was get it back to their ship.

The TARDIS stood in a side corridor leading back to the airlock. Since the robots could measure an object with just a glance, they had already confirmed that the time machine would fit through the airlock doors and back into their own ship. So, it should be a simple matter to just drag the box along the corridor, through the airlock and back to their own ship.

The box was made of wood. How heavy could it be?

Very heavy, it turned out.

One robot had tried to move it on his own. He had put both claws against the back of the box and pushed hard, trying to edge it along the corridor. The TARDIS, though, hadn't budged an inch. The robot moved round to the other side of the box, grasped the corners and tried to drag it away. But still, the machine would not move.

So, the robot called a couple of his friends across. They surrounded the TARDIS but, despite a combination of shoves and pulls and heaves and thrusts, they too utterly failed to move it!

In the end, it took half a dozen robots to finish the job. They were some of the Eternal Victory's biggest and burliest robots, too!

Although it looked like a simple wooden cabinet, the TARDIS obviously hid many secrets inside. The robots could not wait to open the time machine's doors and reveal its treasures…

The other robots led their prisoners into the dark, grimy interior of their warship. Amy, Rory, the Doctor, Sam and Messy were taken along a long, low corridor. The walls were oily and black, and they were braced with thick metal buttresses. Here and there, gouts of steam hissed violently out of pressure valves, filling the corridor with a cool mist that smelt of metal. As they walked, herded by the robots and the guns they wielded, their footsteps clanged noisily on the wire-mesh floor. One corridor on the warship looked much like another, so, although they had walked for little more than a minute, Amy was already totally lost by the time they arrived at the security wing.

There was no door separating the cells from the rest of the ship, just a narrow passage, wide enough for two people at most. Beyond this passage lay a more open room, which seemed just as gloomy, dirty and smelly as everywhere else on the warship. The room was ringed with half a dozen cells, each one with a door made of thick, metal bars. In the centre of the room, Amy saw a strange chair. It looked like a madman's idea of a dentist's chair: it was made of steel, but it was rusted with age and covered with years' worth of dirt. Thick fabric straps hung down from its edges, each fitted with a heavy metal buckle.

Amy watched helplessly as the robots strapped the Doctor into the chair. The robots then turned to her, Rory and Sam, using their guns to usher them into a single cell. They locked the door behind them and then, happy their prisoners were safely confined, the robots marched briskly out of the security wing.

The robots had thrown Messy into the cell with them, accusing the little robot of being a traitor to the Empire of Eternal Victory. He sulked silently in the corner, his one arm drooping down at his side.

Commander Zero-1 loomed over the helpless Doctor. 'Before we begin,' he said, 'I have a few more questions about the spider.'

The Doctor held the robot's gaze with a steely glare. Amy knew he would rather do anything than cooperate with Zero-1, but she realised that he had little choice in the matter.

'How does it make diamond out of nothing?' the robot asked.

'It doesn't,' the Doctor said. 'Well, it makes diamond, yes, but not out of nothing. The spider eats metal for nutrition, but that's not all it eats. It also chews asteroid rock.'

'Rocks which contain a lot of carbon,' the robot added.

The Doctor nodded. 'Exactly. It digests the carbon and uses it to make its diamond webs.'

'Most ingenious,' said Zero-1 as he paced the room. He seemed deep in thought. 'If we could find a way to mimic that process, we would have an endless supply of diamond. But first, we'd have to experiment on the spider to find out how its web-making organs work.'

The Doctor's face twisted in agony as he strained against the tight bands pinning him to the chair. 'You can't!' he spat. 'I won't let you harm that beautiful creature!'

'I would like to remind you, Doctor,' said Zero-1, 'that you are in no position to argue. When we have the spider in our grasp, we will dissect it and learn its marvellous secrets.'

Amy grasped the bars of her cell. 'You're a *monster*,' she shouted. 'You can't just cut it open!'

Rory gently laid his hands on her shoulders and pulled her away from the cell door. 'Amy,' he said, 'stay calm. There's nothing we can do.'

Zero-1 turned to face her, his red mask set in a fierce grimace. 'Your friend is right – there is *nothing* you can do. The Empire will secure victory at *any* cost,' he said. 'We must continue to grow strong, we must continue to conquer lesser races and weaker worlds. We must improve, we strive to be better. We will take any advantage and make it our own.'

Amy got the feeling he was reciting some sort of code of honour, or a mantra. His belief in his own words seemed almost religious. He silently stared at her for a moment, and Amy could feel the tension in the air.

'I will send a kill squad to disable the spider,' he said at last. 'They will remove the creature's diamond-making organs. In time, we will use them to strengthen our forces. We will cruise the galaxy in diamond-hulled starships. We will wear diamond-toughened armour into battle.'

'This is an outrage,' the Doctor said. His voice was calm and level, but Amy could hear the anger bubbling under the surface. 'Whatever happens, I won't let you get away with this.'

Zero-1 laughed. It was a harsh, electronic noise and it chilled Amy to the bone. 'As I said, Doctor, you have no choice,' he said. 'I will return shortly, once my kill squad has succeeded in their mission.' And with that, he turned and marched out of the room.

Amy's eyes met the Doctor's. She could see he was full of terror for the fate of the diamondweb spider, and gripped by a powerful rage at his inability to help. She squeezed the bars of her cell more tightly.

'We'll get out,' she said to him, her voice soft and reassuring. 'We'll stop them.'

CHAPTER 12
ESCAPE

Like the good crew they were, the crewmembers of the *Black Horizon* had followed their orders and evacuated the ship aboard the escape pods. Each pod could hold half a dozen people, even if things were a little cramped, and they each had a small, circular porthole. The crew were staring through those portholes now, not quite believing the impossible sights they were seeing.

For a start, they could no longer see their ship. Where it had once hung in space, now there was just a gigantic, white cocoon. It looked soft and fluffy, like a cloud, but their sensors told them it was tougher than steel. The ship was now encased in an unbreakable diamond cocoon. And the spider which had wrapped it up was now hovering menacingly over its captured prey.

The crew had to face the facts. The *Black Horizon* was lost.

The spider balanced precariously on the delicate strand of its web, its pinpoint feet gently turning the cocoon this way and that. It seemed to be checking its handiwork, making sure that every square inch of the cocoon was intact. Slowly, it began to pull the ship towards itself, dragging it back in the direction from which the spider had come.

Back to its lair...

But the spider wasn't the only thing moving among the twisting strands of web and the spinning asteroids. A group of tiny shapes had emerged from the Empire's ramshackle starship. No more than half a dozen, they looked like tiny flecks of dust against the black background of the space.

They seemed to drift aimlessly at first, as if

they were nothing more than chunks of garbage discarded from the robots' spaceship. But they suddenly stopped, then all turned to face in the same direction. Then, just as suddenly, the shapes started to move quickly, with purpose, gliding silently through the space between the asteroids.

The watching crewmembers squinted and looked closely at these strange new arrivals. They saw metal bodies glinting in the dim starlight. They saw the menacing glow of light in their mechanical eyes.

The tiny specks of junk were actually a heavily-armed squadron of robots from the Empire of Eternal Victory. And they were closing in on the spider…

Rory had been examining every inch of the cell door for a few minutes now. Amy had watched him as he carefully went about his work. He peered closely at the hinges. He stroked the paintwork, feeling for imperfections. He tapped the joints where the bars had been welded into the door's framework. Finally, he stood up and let out a long, deep breath.

'You've no ideas, have you?' Amy said with a wry smile.

Rory coughed uncomfortably. 'None at all. Sorry, Amy.'

She patted him on the shoulder. 'It's okay,' she said, 'the Doctor will figure something out.'

'Oh, *will* I?' the Doctor cried from the room outside. 'I am glad you have some confidence in me, because let me tell you – I have absolutely no idea how to get us out of this one. I am *stumped*.'

Sam stood up, joining Amy and Rory at the door. He whispered to them, quiet enough for the Doctor not to hear. 'I thought you said the Doctor could fix anything?'

'Most of the time, he can,' said Amy. 'Don't worry, Sam, something will come up.'

Rory punched the metal bars in frustration. 'Ow,' he said, 'that hurt.' He shook his sore hand.

'Come on, boys,' said Amy, her gaze passing from Rory to the Doctor to Sam. 'We can think of something! Let's start with the door. What do we know about it? It's metal, and it's pretty solid, if Rory's bruised hand is anything to go by. We've got bars, and none of us are strong enough to bend them. Okay, okay…'

'The lock is pretty advanced,' said Sam, pointing at the computer panel embedded in the wall next to the door. 'I doubt we can crack that, even if we could reach it.'

The Doctor groaned in frustration, straining against his bonds. 'If only I had a free hand, I could use the sonic screwdriver.'

Time seemed to suddenly slow down for Amy as she remembered something the Doctor had obviously forgotten. The sonic screwdriver! Of course! 'You couldn't use it,' she said to him.

'Yes, I could,' he replied, a little confused. 'Just a quick *buzz*, and I'd have you out of there in a jiffy.'

'Oh, I'm sure it would work like that,' said Amy, 'but you still couldn't do it. You haven't got the sonic screwdriver.'

'What do you mean? It's in my pocket…'

'Nope,' she said. 'It's in *my* pocket. You dropped it before, when the ship's gravity went haywire. I picked it up, and I never gave it back!'

The Doctor burst into a shining white grin. 'Amy, that's brilliant!'

She started to fish the device out of her jacket pocket, when a sudden thought occurred to the Doctor. 'Oh, hang on, though – hang on! If we go waving around tech like that in the security wing, we'll set off all sorts of alarms.'

'This is true,' said Messy. 'This is a high security zone, and the usage of advanced technology would alert the guards. They would confiscate the device.'

'And we can't have that!' the Doctor said. 'The sonic screwdriver is our trump card. Messy, my little friend, I need to know: what kind of technology can we use in here without alerting the guards?'

'Only technology owned by the Empire of Eternal Victory is authorised for use in the security wing.'

The Doctor smiled. 'Technology such as your good self?'

Messy whirred and juddered back and forth on his wheels. 'I don't understand.'

'What kind of security clearance do you have, Messy?'

The little robot jiggled back and forth, clearly agitated. 'Security clearance?' he warbled. 'What do you mean?'

'I mean,' said the Doctor, his patience wearing thin, 'can you open the cell door? Do you know how? Are you even *allowed*?'

'Oh, no, no, no!' said Messy. The robot quivered in fear. 'I would be dismantled if I tampered with the security arrangements aboard this ship! I am just a simple plumbing-bot!'

Amy had a thought. A mischievous smile crossed her face as she crouched down next to Messy. She rapped his boxy metal head with her knuckles. 'Listen up, sunshine,' she said. 'Why do you think they've thrown you in jail with us? Your robotic friends think you're a traitor – so you're probably going to be dismantled anyway! But if you help us…'

Messy quivered in fear, his loose nuts and bolts rattling noisy. 'Dismantled?' he stammered.

'Not necessarily,' Amy said. 'If you help us, we can all escape, beat the bad guys and live to see another day. So, how about it? Reckon you can pop open the door?'

Messy was silent for a few moments. 'I... I really can't. I'm not lying – I just don't have the ability. The locks are too complex,' he said. 'But...'

'But what?' called the Doctor from outside. '*What?* Come on, Messy!'

'There are ventilation ducts running throughout the ship,' Messy explained.

'Ventilation? Like, for air?' Rory said, confused. 'But robots don't breathe. Why do you need air?'

Messy turned his head, taking in their surroundings. 'This ship may look brand new,' he said, 'but it is thousands of years old, as old as the Empire itself. Once upon a time, it belonged to the original warriors of the Eternal Victory – and, as they were *living* beings, they did need air to breathe. The plumbing-bots were responsible for the maintenance and upkeep on the ventilation system, as well as all the pipes on the ship.

'As we conquered more and more of our enemies and stole their technology,' Messy continued, 'the ship evolved into what you see today. But the bones of the original spaceship are still there – including the ventilation ducts.'

'Of course,' said the Doctor. 'That explains why *we* can breathe.'

The robot nodded. 'We leave them active, for those occasions where we need to keep organic beings on-board. As our... pr... pris...' Messy couldn't get the word out.

'There's no need to be nervous about it,' said the Doctor with a laugh. 'We're *all* prisoners today!'

'So then, Messy, what are you saying?' Amy said, kneeling down to stare him in the eye. 'Is there a way into this ventilation system?'

Messy rolled over to the wall and pointed at a metal grille. It was set into the wall, about six inches off the ground. It was the size of a small window, just big enough for someone to crawl through. 'This is a vent,' he said. 'Behind it, there is a shaft that leads into the whole network of ducts throughout the ship.'

Amy smiled. 'And do you think you could open it?'

'Certainly,' he replied. He even sounded a little pleased with himself.

'Excellent,' said the Doctor. 'Now then, Amelia. Pay attention. I need you to be very brave…'

CHAPTER 13
ABYSS

The only thing the spider cared about was its dinner. It was hunched over the cocooned form of the *Black Horizon*, its legs bunched tightly around its prey. Its mandibles glinted, wet and white, as they teased the soft edges of the cocoon. It looked almost as if the spider was tasting what it had caught.

The giant creature was so absorbed by its prey that it failed to see the five silver spots drifting through space towards it.

The robots were closing in, their approach stealthy and silent in the vacuum of space. Their eyes – black, soulless camera lenses – were focused tightly on their target. Their masks, glittering in the light from Gloriana XVI, were set in grim, determined glowers. Each one wore a jetpack on its back, and tiny jets of blue flame propelled them through the vacuum towards the spider.

One robot, larger than the others, pulled in front of his fellows to take the lead. The others fell in behind, making a 'V' shape, like an arrowhead pointing straight at their prey. The leader lifted a bulky rifle in its arms and took aim...

A bolt of fiery red energy tore across space, smashing into the spider's thick carapace. Chunks of bony material spiralled chaotically into the darkness. But the spider itself didn't react – it barely noticed the attack. It was just a tiny scratch in its skin.

The robots were fixed in their arrowhead formation, and they continued to move slowly and steadily towards the spider. All five now raised their guns and opened fire...

Sam carefully placed the grille back over the open

hatch, letting Messy roll in to close the clasps that kept it fixed to the wall. He stood and turned to the Doctor. 'Are you sure they're going to be all right?' he said.

The Doctor held his gaze, giving him his best reassuring look. 'They'll be fine. They've got each other, remember.'

Sam nodded. 'I suppose you're right,' he said, but the uncertainty was clear in his voice. 'What happens if the robots come back, though? They're going to notice that two of their prisoners have suddenly gone missing.'

'Well,' said the Doctor, swallowing nervously, 'we'll cross that bridge when we come to it.'

Sam gazed down at the grille once more, gripped with worry.

Amy was on all fours, crawling through the dusty metal tubes in the heart of the robots' spaceship. She thought the idea of ventilation ducts was that they carried fresh air from place to place. So, why did this one feel so hot and stuffy? The narrow shaft was dark and filled with the noise of distant, rumbling engines. The air here smelt dry and grimy. Amy felt like she was crawling through the belly of some giant metal dragon.

She wiped her brow and stopped to catch her breath. Behind her, she heard Rory shuffle to a halt as well. 'Are you okay?' he asked.

'Fine,' Amy said. 'How much further do you think it is?'

'Well, Messy said it was only a hundred metres or so,' Rory said. 'We must be nearly there.'

They were looking for the TARDIS. Messy had explained that all new technology stolen by the crew was first taken to a special laboratory in the heart of the ship. There, each new machine was tested, so the robots could find out everything about it. Messy was sure that's where they would find the Doctor's time machine.

'Look,' said Amy, 'up ahead.' She pointed ahead of her, to where a beam of dappled light pierced the gloom inside the duct. 'That looks like it could be another grille.'

There was just one problem: between them and the grille lay an abyss. Just a few metres in front of Amy, the floor of the shaft fell away, leaving a gap of a couple of metres ahead of them. Amy guessed it must be a junction in the ventilation system, taking air down to the levels below them. Amy shuffled carefully forward, to peer over the edge of the drop. She could just about see the bottom, but it was a long way down. A hiss of steam gushed up from the gloom below, and Amy dodged back quickly to avoid it, knocking into Rory.

She apologised to him, then stared across the gap again. 'How are we going to get over?'

Rory edged around to join her at the ledge. The two of them were now packed quite tightly next to each other in the cramped shaft. He puffed up his cheeks and blew out the air, shaking his head. 'I've no idea,' he said. 'Couldn't we jump it?'

'We'd need to do a running jump to cross that,' she pointed out, 'and we can't stand up, so how would we run?'

'Good point. Clever wife.'

The two of them stared at the gap for a few, long seconds, completely flummoxed. There was no way to jump it, and no way to climb over either – the walls of the shaft were smooth, with nothing to grip on to.

Amy felt Rory tense up, then he whispered, ever so quietly, 'I think we've got another problem, too.' He pointed downwards, into the misty murk beneath them.

Amy looked down, following the line of his finger, and saw a little cluster of purple lights among the clouds of steam. The lights were growing steadily brighter, and Amy could just about hear the clink and clank of robotics. As the clouds of steam parted, she saw a small, squat machine – about the size of an armchair – slowly working its way up the shaft.

The machine didn't look like the other robots – it had no mask for a start, and no obvious face on which to wear it! The robots Amy had met had all been humanoid, with arms and legs, but this was little more than a stocky cube-shaped contraption. It was supported by sucker-like feet which stuck out from its sides. They popped and plopped in and out, pulling the robot slowly up the shaft. It made a humming, whirring noise as it went – it sounded a bit like a Hoover.

'I think,' Amy said, 'that it's just some sort of cleaning machine.'

Rory glanced nervously at her, then back at the approaching machine. 'Are you sure? How do you tell the difference? I mean, I know it's not the time to bring it up, but I can't remember the last time I saw you doing housework…'

Amy glared at Rory, then leant slowly forward over the edge. 'Hello?' she called, her voice quite loud. The machine made no response. It just carried on popping and whirring as it got higher and higher in the shaft. 'Well, if it were one of the other robots – you know, the murderous ones with the scary faces – I don't think it would be ignoring us right now. No, I think it just works its way around these shafts keeping them clean. Oh,' she said suddenly. 'I think I've had an idea.'

Rory's face fell. 'Your ideas usually end with someone ending up in big trouble.'

'Well, we're in pretty big trouble as it is,' she pointed out. 'Look, just get ready to move the second I tell you to…'

Rory looked at the climbing machine, then back at Amy, then across the gap – and he suddenly realised what she had in mind. He gulped. 'You can't be serious,' he said, his voice uneasy.

The machine was nearly level with the floor of the shaft now. 'I'm being very serious,' Amy said, bracing herself against the wall, ready to move. With a final *plop*, the machine had risen high enough to completely close the gap that Rory and Amy had to cross. 'Now!' she yelled, and she threw herself forward, pushing away from the wall.

The cleaning machine wobbled a little as Amy clambered across its top, but it stayed pretty solid. She reached the other side of the gap in just a few seconds, then whizzed around to check on Rory. He was still nervously waiting at the other side, clearly terrified about using the robot as a bridge.

'Rory,' Amy snapped, 'come on. Quickly!' But still he hesitated. The robot was rising now, and soon it would fill the gap between them. 'You've got to move *now*!'

Amy held her hand out towards him, beckoning him, urging him to move. She saw him swallow nervously once and then, with his eyes closed, he leapt forward. Amy grabbed for him, bunching a handful of his shirt in her fist and dragging it hard towards her. The two of them tumbled backwards, a jumble of arms and legs, landing uncomfortably further along the shaft.

Amy quickly looked back, and sighed with relief when she saw the cleaning robot whirring its way away from them, back the way they had come. 'It's okay,' she said to Rory. 'We're safe. We made it!'

He quickly pulled himself together, collapsing

back against the wall of the shaft and catching his breath. He looked at Amy and smiled. 'That was close.'

'Yeah,' she said, 'but without our little cleaning friend, we wouldn't have got here. Look…' She pointed behind her, towards the grille which was now only a little distance away. 'Come on, we're nearly there.'

Amy started to move forward again, sliding her knees along the smooth metal beneath her. Rory followed quickly, and before long they reached the grille.

Amy checked the frame and found the clasps holding it in place. Carefully, she pulled them back, one by one, then removed the grille. She placed it down next to her, wincing when the metal grille scraped noisily on the floor of the shaft.

Carefully, inch by agonising inch, Amy poked her head through the hole and looked down into the room below her. There was the TARDIS! Big and blue and like a long-lost friend. She grinned and whispered to Rory, 'There it is!'

The TARDIS stood in the centre of the laboratory. It was a big, bright room – the cleanest room she'd seen so far. The walls were white, and the floor was a shiny sheet of steel. Rows and rows of shelves lined the walls; these were full of dozens of pieces of half-dismantled technology. The robots' spoils of war. At one end of the room, there was a big, white table, which was full of odds and ends. Two robots stood by the table, each poking and prodding at the machinery spread out before them.

They picked up each piece of technology, one by one, and raised it up to their microscope eyes. They turned it this way and that, peering at each piece from every angle. Then, they turned to their computers, tapped in some data, and put the trinket to one side. Then they picked up the next piece of technology and started the whole process all over again.

Every now and again, they would scowl and throw one of the devices on to a pile of discarded technology on the floor. This pile of broken and burnt-out machinery was clearly no use to them – it was just rubbish. But Amy's eyes lit up when she saw it. She had an idea…

CHAPTER 14
SALVAGE

In the security wing, the Doctor's ears pricked up. He could hear metal footsteps rattling quickly along the corridor outside, and his blood ran cold. If the robots discovered that Rory and Amy were missing, the whole plan could fall apart…

'Sam,' the Doctor hissed, 'no matter what happens, I want you to stay very, very calm.'

Sam leapt up, grasping the bars of his cell. 'Why? What's happening?'

The Doctor strained against his bonds once more, but it was still useless. He was stuck tight. 'Just keep quiet. Trust me. It's all going to be fine.'

At that moment, two robots appeared in the

doorway. They took up positions either side of the door, flanking the exit like guards. They each held a nasty-looking rifle with a glowing red crystal fixed at the tip of the barrel. Their angular masks were set in gruesome grimaces, and their eyes shone a fierce red.

'Hello there,' said the Doctor. He flashed a friendly smile at the robots. 'It's so lovely to have some visitors. I was just saying to Sam – wasn't I, Sam? – that we needed some company. A couple of fresh faces can cheer you right up. Even if the faces are as scary as yours.'

'What are you doing, Doctor?' whispered Sam. 'You don't want to make them mad.'

But the robots didn't react at all. They stood stock still, staring straight ahead, their faces still scowling angrily.

'I don't suppose,' said the Doctor, 'you chaps would consider loosening these restraints, would you?' He waggled his hands, as if to demonstrate the tight plastic bindings around his wrists. 'It's just that I think I'm going to get some nasty pins and needles unless I can get up, stretch my legs, you know…'

Still, the robots stood still and silent.

'No,' said the Doctor with a sigh. 'No, I didn't think so. Oh well.'

There was a moment's pause. Then, one of the robot's heads turned slightly. If the Doctor hadn't been paying attention, he would have missed it. It was the tiniest movement, and he only spotted it because the angles of the robot's mask caught the light in a fractionally different way.

The robot was looking over towards the cell.

The Doctor's two hearts skipped a beat.

He pulled against his restraints again, trying to be as noisy and obvious as he could. 'Seriously now, fellers,' he said. 'I think one of my legs has gone completely dead. Couldn't you just let me out for a minute?'

The robot ignored him. It took a few steps towards the cell instead, its head tipping quizzically to one side.

'Honestly, I'm in agony!' the Doctor cried.

'Have some sympathy!'

The robot stopped moving. It stared into the cell, and Sam stared back, the colour draining from his face. 'I… we're sorry, we just…' he stammered. 'Hello, um…'

'Where,' said the robot, in a slow, deep voice, 'are the other two prisoners? The human male and the female?'

'They just, um… they just popped out for some fresh air,' said Sam. He winced at the weakness of his excuse.

The robot stared at him for a second, then suddenly spun on its heel. It crossed back to the door and leant into the corridor outside. It slammed a big, red button on the door frame and a siren started to blare out all around the ship.

'Commander!' the robot guard yelled, its metallic voice ringing out along the corridor. 'Commander! The prisoners have escaped!'

Amy pointed at the heap of junk lying on the floor next to the laboratory table. 'Look at that, Rory,' she said. 'Are you thinking what I'm thinking?'

Rory shuffled a little closer to the hatch and looked down into the room. 'I don't know what you're thinking, but I think it's just a pile of rubbish.'

'Yeah, but what *kind* of rubbish?'

Rory looked again, confusion clouding his face. '*Rubbish* rubbish?'

Amy gave an impatient 'huff!' and pointed straight downwards into the room. 'The TARDIS is just there, right below us,' she said. 'But we can't just drop down and hop in – those robots would raise the alarm as soon as they saw us. We need a distraction.'

She fished around in the pocket of her jacket then pulled out the sonic screwdriver. 'This,' she said, 'is the answer to our prayers. When I tell you, I need you to drop straight down on to the roof of the TARDIS, okay? I'll come straight down after you.'

Rory nodded, swallowing nervously. Amy smiled reassuringly, then held the sonic screwdriver out, pointing it straight at the pile of discarded machinery on the floor below.

She had seen the screwdriver in action a million times – and yet, now it was in her hands, it suddenly seemed a lot more complicated than the Doctor made it look. She looked for a switch or a button but couldn't find any. She shook it, but nothing happened. Gripping it tightly, she flicked the device hard. The screwdriver's top popped open like an eagle's claw, and it started emitting a high-pitched whine. She aimed its green light down at the pile of junk and hoped for the best.

Among the cast-offs, Amy was sure she'd seen things that looked like robotic limbs – arms and legs, claws and pincers, wheels and tracks. All the useless, old, broken parts that the robots had thrown away. But they weren't quite *totally* broken...

With a rusty creaking noise, the pile of machinery started to twitch. Scraps of metal clattered to the floor. Various technological doodahs rolled noisily aside as the discarded robot parts leapt into action. Steel-fingered hands grasped at thin air, legs waved in a mockery of motion, and arms floundered on the floor like grounded fish. The whole mass made a tangled, twisted scraping noise.

The laboratory's little scrapyard had sprung to life! It was the perfect diversion. The two robots yelped in shock, backing away from the living mess of metal by their table. It was the perfect time to move – when the robots were looking elsewhere.

Amy leant to one side, leaving the hatch open for Rory. 'Now,' she said. 'Go, quickly!'

Rory hurriedly shoved past her, dropping down on to the TARDIS's roof as quietly as he could. He then slid down on to the floor and, once Amy saw that he was safely on the ground, she followed him. While the robots squawked in panic, Amy and Rory slipped silently into the TARDIS…

Commander Zero-1 stood in the doorway to the security wing. His tall, thin form was silhouetted by the light from the corridor outside, making him look like a huge, shadowy skeleton. His mask was set in an expression of anger, and his eyes burned a furious crimson. Sam was suddenly thankful to be stuck behind the bars of his cell – at least they might offer some protection if Zero-1 flew into a rage!

The robot took two heavy steps into the room, his feet clanging loudly on the floor. 'Where have the others gone?' he boomed. 'How did they escape?'

The Doctor stayed infuriatingly calm. He just smiled back at Zero-1 and said, 'You need to check out your security, mate. The Empire of the Eternal Victory, the most technologically advanced warmongers in the universe, and you can't keep a couple of weak old humans safely locked up!'

Zero-1 was silent. He barely moved, but his face mask shifted, the mouth turning downwards in a frown of anger. When Zero-1 spoke, his voice was quiet and menacing. 'We will find your friends and when we do, we will see if you're still smiling then. But for now, I think it's time we started to extract the information about your time machine.'

With his two guards falling into step behind him, Zero-1 started to march slowly towards the Doctor...

CHAPTER 15
RESCUE

Amy looked down at the TARDIS console and, for the first time, it looked frightening and confusing. She was used to thinking of its shiny glass and multi-coloured lights as friendly and clever little things. The Doctor could pull a lever, flick a switch or twist a dial, and the TARDIS would go whooshing off to their next adventure. Now and again, Amy would help him at the controls, holding down a lever or pushing two buttons at once, but she was only doing what the Doctor told her to do – she had no idea what any of this stuff actually did!

'What now?' asked Rory. 'What did the Doctor

say we had to do?'

Before they'd broken out of the cell, the Doctor had given Amy and Rory a very simple, clear set of instructions. And, as this was only a very short trip, he had reassured them that there was very little that could go wrong.

Even so, Amy chewed her lip nervously.

'Find the row of six red buttons on the side of the console nearest to the door,' the Doctor had said. Once Amy had found them, she clicked down the first and second, as the Doctor had instructed. She then had to wiggle the zigzag plotter four times, and throw the big black lever to its left.

As the lever slammed home, the TARDIS shuddered and wheezed into life. The lights in the control room flickered, then glowed more warmly, and the balloon-like glass structure in the time rotor started to glide up and down, up and down. She checked the old-fashioned TV monitor overhead. A series of green numbers were flashing quickly by. They were moving too quickly to read, but that was okay – the Doctor had simply said, 'As long as the numbers are green, everything is fine. If they go purple, then we've got problems...'

Amy knew they had to move quickly now. 'Rory, you're up!'

Rory dashed to the opposite side of the console and pulled a set of blue-handled sliders all the way down towards him. The TARDIS jerked to one side and the movement sent Rory flying. He stumbled towards a flight of steps but managed to grab hold of the handrail just in time.

'Okay!' he said, catching his breath. 'That doesn't usually happen.'

Finally, Amy punched the mushroom-like dome on a big, red button and – with a whoosh, a clang and a heavy thud – the TARDIS materialised.

With a clatter and a bang, Zero-1 crashed into the big blue box that had suddenly appeared in front of him. Confused and angry, he staggered backwards. His guards moved quickly to stop him from falling flat on his metal backside. With a cry of rage, Zero-1 lashed out, hitting the Doctor's time machine with his fists.

'What trickery is this?' he yelled.

Safely on the other side of the TARDIS, the Doctor burst out laughing with joy. 'Ponds to the rescue!' he cried, his voice full of pride and triumph.

Across the room, watching from his cell, Sam's eyes were as wide as dinner plates. 'What is *that*?'

The TARDIS doors swung open and Amy – followed by a slightly giddy-looking Rory – flew out. 'We did it!' she yelled.

'My wife, the time-space pilot!' said Rory with a laugh.

'Come here, you…' She grabbed hold of Rory's lapels and gave him a big, soppy kiss.

'When you two have *quite* finished,' the Doctor said with mock impatience, 'if you could point the sonic screwdriver at these restraints here, I would be *ever* so grateful.'

Amy pulled the sonic from her pocket and waved it at the Doctor. 'I don't know how to work this thing,' she said, her fingers poking and prodding the device, 'I think I just got lucky before…'

There was a sudden, sharp whirring noise and the straps holding down the Doctor's wrists and ankles popped open. He leapt off the table and swept Amy into a huge hug. 'You are amazing,' he said. He snatched the sonic from her grasp and pointed it casually towards the cell door, which swung open. Sam and Messy dashed out, thanking the Doctor profusely.

The Doctor was standing by the open TARDIS door. From the other side of the TARDIS, they could hear Zero-1 roaring with anger, his fists thump-thump-thumping on the side of the ship.

'Come on everyone, get inside, quickly,' the Doctor said. 'We've got a spider to save…'

As the TARDIS faded away in a swirl of dust and debris, Commander Zero-1's failure was revealed. The table where the Doctor had been tied down was now empty. The cell, too, was empty, its door swinging open. Zero-1 screamed in fury, his mask shifting into an expression of pain and rage.

His prisoners had escaped and with them, any hope of getting his hands on the Time Lords' fabled technology.

He swung to face the two guards standing at his side. 'Gather the troops,' he growled. 'I want every able-bodied solider ready to launch into space on my command.'

'Yes, sir,' they replied. 'What are your orders?'

Zero-1's face mask darkened a shade, the eyebrows knotting ominously.

'I have already sent a small squadron to kill the spider – but it's taking too long,' he said. 'Every soldier is to get out there now, and they are not to come back until that creature is destroyed. Tear it to pieces and bring me whatever's left.'

CHAPTER 16
SURROUNDED

The robots of the Empire of Eternal Victory came pouring out of the warship in their hundreds. They looked like a huge cloud of tiny, silver flies, swarming through the vacuum towards the unsuspecting spider. They carried an assortment of weapons, all of which they were ready to use against the creature. Some robots carried simple, efficient blaster rifles. Others carried knives and saws and all manner of cutting equipment. Others still were laden down with surgical lasers and hyper-scalpels, ready to carve out the most valuable parts of the spider's body.

The spider, however, barely noticed them

coming. The robots' kill squad, the five soldiers who had already blown a chunk out of its carapace, were certainly too tiny for the spider to even notice. The same five now hovered right by the spider's huge, bulbous abdomen, bringing their weapons to bear in an effort to slice the creature open. But they weren't having much luck: the spider's exoskeleton was impossibly tough, and though they could scratch and scar the surface, they showed little sign of being able to cut through.

But no matter – they had seen the horde of their fellow robots tearing through space to join them. And leading the charge, their brave warlord, Commander Zero-1. His eyes blazed white, and his face mask shone with the glory of impending victory.

With the whole might of their forces ranged against this one, stupid animal, there could be no doubt: the Empire of the Eternal Victory would triumph again.

The Doctor tore open the TARDIS door and peered out into space. Behind him, Sam gasped in shock. Amy patted him on the shoulder and smiled. 'Don't worry,' she said, 'it's perfectly safe. You can even float about outside – not that I would recommend it…'

'But… but…' Sam was stammering in confusion. 'How does it do that? How does the air stay inside?' Sam stared wildly this way and that. 'And how come it's so much bigger on the inside, anyway? How does it *work*?'

'If it helps,' said Rory, 'I've got no idea either. It's probably just easiest to say "a wizard did it".'

Sam swallowed nervously, took a deep breath and tried to smile.

'Welcome to the TARDIS,' said Amy with a smile. 'It *is* pretty magical.'

The Doctor ignored the conversation going on behind him. He let out a long, deep sigh of wonderment as he took in the full sight outside the ship. 'Amy, Rory,' he said, waving them over. 'All of you, come and look at *this*!'

He flung open the TARDIS's other door, revealing the full vista of the asteroid field. They were hovering high above the whole expanse of rocks now, and could finally see the full extent of the spider's web. It stretched from asteroid to asteroid, straight lines angled around and between the wheeling rocks. Thin, delicate white streaks spreading for miles in every direction. They tangled chaotically around each other and, where the rocks spun, they spun with them – the web constantly weaving itself into complex, unpredictable new patterns.

Amy's eyes were wide in astonishment. 'Wow,' she said. 'I had no idea the web would be that big.'

'It's a big spider, Amy,' the Doctor said. 'Something that eats asteroids for breakfast is going to need a suitably sized web.'

'How big *is* the web?' asked Rory. 'I mean, roughly.'

'I'd say a thousand miles from end to end,' the Doctor said. 'Huge, certainly. *Massive*. But what's clever is how the spider manages to hide it, weaving it in-between the rocks, leaving so few visible traces.'

'But why does it try to hide the web at all?' Amy asked. 'To trap its unsuspecting victims?'

'No,' the Doctor replied. 'Remember, I said it doesn't deliberately eat starships – it's happy with just space rock. It's not hiding the web to trick anyone – it's just covering its tracks. Hiding any evidence of its presence in the asteroid field.' The Doctor looked suddenly sad. 'It knows that there are cruel people in the universe who would hunt it down, to trap it or kill it. It knows it has predators. So it knows it has to stay hidden.'

'Poor thing,' Amy whispered.

'Yes, indeed,' the Doctor said. He took a deep breath and clapped his hands together. 'And that's why it needs our help. Look down there…'

The Doctor pointed across the vast emptiness beneath the TARDIS, to the silvery swarm of robots amassing around the spider. They could see, even from this distance, the occasional red flare of the robots' blaster rifles or the steely glint of a razor-sharp blade.

Messy trundled closer to the open door. 'Our

soldiers,' he said, his voice quiet in horror. 'It looks like just about every one of them, all closing in on the creature.'

Sam, finally getting over his nerves, joined the crowd to look down upon the scene below. 'There's so many of them,' he said. 'How can we ever hope to stop them?'

'Ah,' the Doctor said, grinning. '*We* aren't going to stop them. That spider isn't defenceless, she's just *big*. So big that she barely even notices the great and oh-so-terrifying Empire of Eternal Victory. They're just like little buzzing insects to her.'

Rory laughed. 'Huh, that's ironic. Insects to an insect!'

'Spiders aren't insects, Rory,' the Doctor said without even glancing at him.

Amy rolled her eyes. 'Yeah, Rory,' she said in a mocking tone, 'don't be stupid.' There was a moment's awkward silence before she asked the Doctor, 'They're arachnids, right?'

'That's right,' he said with a smile. '*Anyway*. The

spider isn't defenceless. Look at her! How could a thing that big not be a bit handy in a fight? All we need to do is let her know that she's under attack.'

'How are we going to do that?' Sam asked.

'Shout really, really loudly?' Amy added.

The Doctor smiled, pulling the sonic screwdriver from his pocket. Holding on to the doorframe, he leant out perilously far into space. 'Something like that,' he said – and that was the last thing Amy heard from him before he let go and dropped suddenly out of view!

CHAPTER 17
COMMUNICATION

In the distance, far below the TARDIS, the swirling cloud of robot warriors had finally closed in on the spider. They surged over its whole body in waves, buzzing this way and that, their weapons flashing in the starlight. Slowly, the spider began to react, its massive bulk rippling in the dark. But it almost looked like it was too late. The robots were smothering the creature now, and there seemed no way for it to escape its fate.

The Doctor, though, knew better. He stood high above the spider and her would-be killers, balancing carefully on one foot, wobbling on a thin strand of web. The TARDIS was behind him, the doors still open. Amy hung out from the door, clinging tightly to the doorframe, a desperate look on her face. 'What are you doing?' she cried down at him. 'You're going to get yourself killed!'

'I'm perfectly all right, Amy,' the Doctor called back, see-sawing his arms like a tightrope walker. 'I've extended the TARDIS's atmospheric bubble, so I've got air and gravity down here. I'm fine.'

'Fine?' she said, her voice shrill. 'You're in the middle of an asteroid field perched on a flimsy piece of spider web!'

'It's hardly flimsy,' he said, bouncing experimentally on the tip of his toes. 'Diamond. Stronger than steel, and more beautiful than the stars.'

Rory popped his head out of the TARDIS door, too, boggling at the Doctor's bravery. 'Look,' he said, 'could you save the poetry for another time? You're making me nervous. Just do whatever it is you need to do down there, and let's get moving!'

The Doctor crouched down, balancing carefully on the web. 'You're quite right, Rory, there's no time to waste!' And then he did the strangest thing...

He took out the sonic screwdriver but, just for once, he didn't switch it on. It didn't make its usual buzzing noise, nor did it light up with its usual emerald green colour. He just smiled at it, then used it to tap once, quite firmly, against the diamond thread on which he was balanced.

The Doctor's other hand was held flat against the web, like he was feeling for something. Using the screwdriver, he tapped the web again – once more, then twice, then again and again, more and more rapidly in a strange, scattershot rhythm. As the tapping sped up, the Doctor closed his eyes and fell into a deep, trancelike concentration.

The spider's chitinous shell had withstood much of the robots' attack – until now. Under the relentless blaster bolts and flashing, slicing blades, little chips and chunks of her carapace were flying this way and that, whirling off into space.

And yet, still, she didn't seem to react. She barely seemed to notice her attackers were there at all...

After a few moments, Amy whispered to Rory, 'Is he okay?'

Rory, his face blank, just stared down at their Time Lord friend. The Doctor was still crouched on the web, his eyes closed, tapping away in that strange, unpredictable rhythm. 'Well,' he said, 'the Doctor isn't exactly famous for acting sane. Who knows what this is all about?'

Sam came up behind them, joining them at the open doors. 'You know the Doctor better than I do,' he said uncertainly, 'but that tapping...'

Amy turned to face him. 'You think you know what it is?'

'Well, not precisely,' Sam replied. 'But I think I can guess what *kind* of thing it is. Have you ever heard of Morse code?'

'Like dots and dashes?' Rory said.

Sam nodded. 'I think he's communicating with the spider,' he said. 'I mean, I don't know how exactly – but if it can feel the vibrations in its web, and if they're a particular type of vibration... maybe. I dunno. It's just a thought.'

Amy smiled. 'It's a good thought,' she said. 'That's how spiders know they've caught something in their webs – the prey shaking the web as they try to escape. And the Doctor did say he was going to let her know she was under attack. It makes sense.'

They watched the Doctor in silence for just a few more seconds before they saw a result. Far below, the spider raised her front two legs, slowly and deliberately, high above her head. She stretched them out as far as they would go, far to either side of her body, reaching for two strands of web threaded across a cluster of larger asteroids. Her pinpoint feet brushed the strands, seeming then to grab them fast. Then she started to draw her legs in, pulling the web with them. The asteroids started to move too, the huge rocks gliding faster and faster through space.

Then, the spider reached for different strands of web, this time with four of her legs. She tugged at those too, and more rocks started to spin in a dizzying dance through space.

The web on which the Doctor was standing

shuddered. It rocked violently and he had to fling both arms out to keep his balance.

Amy fell to the floor, hanging out from the TARDIS, stretching her arms out to reach him. 'Doctor!' she screamed. 'Grab hold! Quickly!'

As the web shifted under his feet once again, the Doctor leapt towards Amy – just in time, too. The strand suddenly lurched away, dragging a string of small rocks with it. The Doctor's hands landed in Amy's, and she dragged him quickly inside.

The two of them collapsed in a heap just inside the door, the Doctor laughing as he tried to catch his breath. He quickly scrambled back to the door and gazed down at the spider.

'That's my girl,' he whispered.

The spider was moving quickly now, and getting quicker still. Her sudden, swift motions were already beginning to dislodge the robots. Some of them desperately tried to cling on to her shell; others were flung off her body, wheeling through space like spinning tops.

Her legs flew this way and that, strumming strand after strand of her web, like some manic harpist. Finally, the full extent of her web became visible: the whole asteroid field was full of threads, no longer hidden. The spider was weaving them now, crossing thread with thread in a complicated, rapid dance. And, as the threads criss-crossed each other more and more tightly, the rocks to which they were attached began to spin. Round and round they went, bumping and crashing against each other in a chaotic, dangerous flurry.

Spinning wildly out of control, the robots found themselves pummelled by the circling rocks. Boulder after boulder crashed into their metallic bodies, and they were sent brutally to their dooms, their shattered carcasses smoking and sparking as they were crushed by the rocks or sent flying off in all directions.

Realising the sudden danger they were in, a few of them tried to beat a hasty retreat. But the Doctor had warned the spider well, and she knew what to look for. She wasn't going to let any of her enemies escape so easily.

The spider lashed out, her legs whipping so quickly they glinted like laser beams against the dark of space. She grabbed robot after robot, smashing them against the bigger asteroids or batting them, sending them flying off into oblivion. A few robots ventured too close to her sharp, sparkling mandibles: she lunged at them, grabbing them hungrily in her mouth and swallowing them whole.

There was panic and fear in the lenses of the robot's digital eyes, and their face masks were set in silent screams of terror. But, just as they had shown the spider not an ounce of mercy, she spared them none either.

Commander Zero-1 halted his approach. His troops were shattered and routed. He watched in shock as the surviving members of the Empire scooted off to safety. He had never witnessed such a total, inescapable defeat before. He was used to victory, but he had watched in stunned amazement as the spider suddenly sprang into action, crushing almost all his soldiers within a minute. Now, his only option was to retreat – head back to the ship, gather his battered soldiers and consider his next move.

There, in the distance, spinning like a little metal toy, was the last great warship of the Empire of Eternal Victory. His final bastion, and his only hope of escape.

He activated his jetpack, increasing his speed, and aimed straight for his ship.

Slowly, ever so slowly, the ship started to grow in his vision as he drew closer to it. Soon, soon, he would be safe.

As he glided through the icy space, he started to mutter to himself. He could hear the panic rising in his voice, the manic hysteria in its tone. All he could think about was escape. Escape and survival.

'What will I do?' he wondered. 'I will have to rebuild the Empire. I shall take what survivors I can from this defeat. I shall withdraw and we shall regroup, gather our strength – and then strike back.

Yes, we shall return, even stronger than before, and we shall *strike back…*'

His dreams of revenge clouded his mind with a cold, dark rage. It was all he could think about, he couldn't concentrate on anything else.

Which was unfortunate for him – because, right at that moment, another tug on the spider's web sent an asteroid the size of a double-decker bus swinging slowly into his path.

If Commander Zero-1 had been thinking clearly, he would have seen the rock. If he'd been looking where he was going, he would easily have noticed it and steered himself out of the way.

'Revenge!' he shrieked. '*We shall have revenge!*'

If Commander Zero-1 hadn't been consumed with wicked thoughts of vengeance, he wouldn't have flown straight into the side of the asteroid and been shattered into a million pieces.

In the cold, dark silence of space, as the asteroid glided impassively away, Commander Zero-1's cracked face mask went spinning off, frozen in one final look of furious surprise. As it drifted away, to be lost and forgotten in the cold depths between the stars, so died the dreams of the Empire of Eternal Victory, caught in one final moment of eternal defeat.

CHAPTER 18
PROMISE

It had taken him a little time, but the Doctor had visited each one of the *Black Horizon*'s escape pods, one by one, and transported the human crewmembers safely to the Empire of Eternal Victory's warship. Now, a little dazed and shaken, the crew were trying to get used to their new temporary home. They still had a job to do, after all, as Captain Jones was quick to remind them.

The medical equipment was safely stored in the warship's hold, and the ship itself functioned perfectly well. Sam had carefully examined the engine systems and he had reported that, in fact, the warship was probably significantly faster than the *Black Horizon*. With any luck, they'd be able to easily make up the time they'd lost by being caught in the spider's web and by being attacked by the Empire. They'd be able to get their cargo to its destination in plenty of time.

On the bridge of the warship, Captain Jones shook the Doctor's hand. 'I would like to thank you, Doctor,' she said, 'and your friends. Without you… well, I dread to think what might have happened to us.'

The Doctor smiled. 'It was our pleasure, Captain,' he said.

Amy stepped forward and hugged a rather surprised Sam. 'It was nice to meet you,' she said. 'You look after yourself.' She glanced at the captain, a mischievous glint in her eye. 'I'd say this guy was next in line for a promotion, wouldn't you?'

Captain Jones looked at Sam, letting the tiniest smile play on her lips. 'A commendation, at the very least,' she said.

Sam blushed, then grinned. 'Yes, Captain,' he stammered. 'Thank you. Thank you, Amy, Rory, Doctor… it was lovely to meet you all, too!' He stumbled off to a nearby console and set to work, trying to make full sense of the Empire's ship.

'Now, there's just two little things still to sort out,' the Doctor said, addressing the captain again. He stepped to one side, revealing the quivering form of Messy cowering behind him. 'First of all, this little feller. You will look after him, won't you, Captain?'

Captain Jones looked a little sceptical.

'I promise you, he's no trouble,' said Rory with a grin.

'I'm not,' said Messy, his voice trembling, 'I'm really not.'

'And surely,' Rory added, 'you've got space in your operation for a tip-top plumbing robot?'

'I am *very* good at ventilation systems,' Messy said, sounding a little more confident. 'Very good indeed.'

'And he did help save the day,' the Doctor

pointed out.

Captain Jones rolled her eyes. 'Okay, fine,' she said with a sigh. 'I guess he can stick around. But if you get in any trouble…' She wagged a finger at him.

Messy whirled up to her, circling her feet like an eager puppy. 'I promise I won't!' he chirped. 'Oh, thank you, thank you!' The robot excitedly buzzed away, nearly knocking over Sam in his enthusiasm to share the news with his new friend.

Amy stared after them, a wry smile on her face. 'They make a lovely couple,' she said with a laugh. 'Come on, Rory. I need a cup of tea and a foot rub. Back to the TARDIS with you!' Amy waved her goodbyes to the captain, Sam and Messy, dragging Rory out of the room.

'And the other thing?' Captain Jones said, looking at the Doctor. 'You said there were two things to sort out.'

The Doctor nodded, his face pale and grave. 'I need you to make me a promise,' he said. His expression was flinty and hard. 'I need you to promise me that you will never, *ever* tell anyone about the spider. And order your crew to do the same.'

The captain considered the Doctor's request in silence for a moment.

'No one must ever find her,' he continued. 'For all I know, she's the only diamondweb spider still in existence. The very last of her kind. If anyone even *suspects* she exists, she will be hunted as a prize or a pet. She must live out the rest of her days in peace, and in freedom.'

The Doctor held Captain Jones' gaze – his dark eyes looked threatening and full of an unspoken menace. Finally, she nodded, slowly but with certainty. 'Of course,' she said. 'I promise. I *swear*. I owe you that much. In fact, I owe you a lot more.'

The Doctor suddenly broke into a beaming smile. 'Ah, don't be silly,' he said, his mood suddenly lighter. 'It was nothing! It was a pleasure – it was even fun!'

Clasping his hands in front of his chest, and

half-bowing, he started to back slowly out of the bridge of the warship, towards the TARDIS. 'It was wonderful to meet you all,' he said as he left. 'Take care, everyone. Take care!'

He reached the door, and shot one last look at the captain. 'A promise,' he whispered, 'is a promise.'

As the last warship of the Empire of Eternal Victory carried its new owners off to unknown horizons, peace and stillness finally fell among the rocks of the Gloriana Scattering.

The asteroids were still now, drifting only with the imperceptible breeze of the universe itself. Here and there, there was a glint of white, a hint of crystalline glimmer – but if you blinked, you'd miss it. In fact, if you were just passing by, you'd have no idea at all that there was anything special about this asteroid field. It would look pretty much like any other empty, desolate corner of space. A pile of dead rocks, nothing more.

Nothing special hid among the shadows.

Nothing sat in the silence, patient and still.
Nothing wove its veiled web among the stardust.
No impossibly giant spiders here. No, not at all.

THE END

DOCTOR WHO

The journey through time and space never ends...
For more exciting adventures, look out for

DOCTOR WHO
2 new adventures

SIGHTSEEING
IN SPACE

DAVID BAILEY   STEVE LYONS

Coming soon...
MONSTROUS MISSIONS and **STEP BACK IN TIME**

WANT MORE ACTION? MORE ADVENTURE? MORE ADRENALIN?

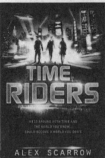

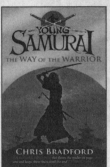

GET INTO PUFFIN'S ADVENTURE BOOKS FOR BOYS